P9-DMU-567

as if being 12³/₄ isn't bad enough, my mother is running for president!

as if being 12³/4 isn't bad enough, my mother is running for president!

DONNA GEPHART

DELACORTE PRESS

Published by Delacorte Press
an imprint of Random House Children's Books
a division of Random House, Inc.
New York

This is a work of fiction. Names, characters, places, and incidents either are the
product of the author's imagination or are used fictitiously.
Any resemblance to actual persons, living or dead, events, or locales
is entirely coincidental.

Copyright © 2008 by Donna Gephart

All rights reserved.

Delacorte Press and colophon are registered trademarks of Random House, Inc.

Visit us on the Web! www.randomhouse.com/kids

Educators and librarians, for a variety of teaching tools,
visit us at www.randomhouse.com/teachers

Library of Congress Cataloging-in-Publication Data
Gephart, Donna.
As if being 12¾ isn't bad enough, my mother is running
for president! / by Donna Gephart.
p cm.
Summary: Preparing for spelling bees, having a secret admirer, and waiting for
her chest size to catch up with her enormous feet are pressure enough, but
twelve-year-old Vanessa must also deal with loneliness and very real fears as her
mother, Florida's Governor, runs for President of the United States.
ISBN: 978-0-385-73481-3 (trade)
ISBN: 978-0-385-90479-7 (library edition) [1. Politics, Practical—Fiction.
2. Mothers and daughters—Fiction. 3. Spelling bees—Fiction. 4. Death
threats—Fiction. 5. Schools—Fiction. 6. Self-confidence—Fiction.
7. Florida—Fiction.] I. Title.
PZ7.G293463As 2008
[Fic]—dc22
2007027601

The text of this book is set in 12-point Goudy.

Printed in the United States of America

10 9 8 7 6 5

First Edition

Random House Children's Books supports the First Amendment
and celebrates the right to read.

Dedicated to Daniel (Daniel. D-A-N-I-E-L. Daniel.) *n*.
1: exceptional husband. 2: fantastic father.
3: guitar-pickin', cold-cereal-chompin', basketball-bouncin',
pun-purveyin' best friend.

Have I told you lately?

ACKNOWLEDGMENTS

With love to my family and friends, who enrich my life every day.

A toast of gratitude with a glass of Ruby Red grapefruit juice to my Sunday group—Linda Salem Marlow, Sylvia Andrews, Carole Crowe, Peter Hawkins, Kieran Doherty, Jill Nadler, Dan Rousseau, and Donald Lovejoy—writers and friends extraordinaire.

A bouquet of thanks to the young readers of my (unwieldy) first draft: Andrew, Paige, and Madelyn.

A shout of thanks to Diahnka Kingsley, talented artist, for sharing her experience of having her broken left wrist set in a purple cast.

Deirdre Flint, hilarious songwriter, is responsible for the idea of a Boob Fairy in this book.

Gracias to Caren Wilder for help with Spanish words and phrases.

A bumblebee pin and a wish for much success to Claire for sharing her spelling bee experiences with me.

Hats off to my editor, Stephanie Lane, and her magic blue editing pencil.

With gratitude to my Scrabble-loving agent, Tina Wexler (T-I-N-A W-E-X-L-E-R), for believing in me and in a quirky character named Vanessa Rothrock. For supporting me from first sentence through final revision, T-H-A-N-K Y-O-U (worth 18 points in Scrabble, but worth even more to me!) for making my dream come true.

The Bee.

I'm sitting on a wooden folding chair, hoping I don't get a splinter in my derriere, as Chester Fields tries to spell "thoroughly." Chester Fields is an idiot. "Thoroughly" is an easy word. But somehow he manages to muck it up, spelling, "T-h-u-r-u-h, I don't know, w-l-y." Cowbell for that boy! How did he even get to the schoolwide bee? I'll bet his teacher felt sorry for him. Or maybe it's because his mother is on the board of directors at Lawndale Academy.

I, Vanessa Rothrock, am sweating like a pig—do pigs sweat?—and wishing I could smell my pits, but the whole audience is looking at me. I pump my left leg up and down like crazy and hear Mom's voice in my head: *Don't fidget, Vanessa; it's unbecoming. Still yourself.* Still yourself? Easy for her to say. She's all poise and grace, forever saying and doing the perfect thing. Maybe I'm not really Mom's daughter.

Maybe I was adopted, or switched at birth. But when I think of Mom's enormous feet, I know I'm all hers. I rest my hand on my leg to stop fidgeting and crane my neck. *Is Mom even—?*

"Vanessa Rothrock, please come up."

I gasp and choke on my own saliva. Then I stand and grab the back of my chair. Unfortunately, I do not die of asphyxiation (Asphyxiation. A-S-P-H-Y-X-I-A-T-I-O-N. Asphyxiation.) and I maneuver around students' feet and chair legs. The microphone is in sight. I'm sighing with relief at having passed through the minefield of legs without tripping when my gigantic feet tangle in the principal's microphone cord.

I lurch forward, grab for the podium, and end up with a handful of papers before crashing to the stage. I say something charming, like "Ooomph!" The audience lets out a collective gasp. Unfortunately, I do not crack my head and die instantly. *Why am I such a klutz?*

As I lift my cheek from the dusty floor, I see camera lights flash like lightning. I put my head down and imagine tomorrow's headline: GOVERNOR'S DAUGHTER TAKES SPILL DURING SCHOOL SPELLING BEE. ENTIRE STATE OF FLORIDA HUMILIATED.

"No photographs, please," Mrs. Foster begs. "You were informed."

I look up again and see Mr. Martinez marching toward me from backstage. That's all I need to complete the humiliation package—my six-foot-tall security guard scooping me up from the stage and brushing me off.

I hold up a few fingers and he stops. I mouth the words "I'm okay." Mr. Martinez backs up so that he's offstage again. And against my better judgment, I stand and face the audience, who, by the way, have their mouths hanging open. My cheeks grow so hot I'm sure my head will spontaneously (Spontaneously. S-P-O-N-T-A-N-E-O-U-S-L-Y. Spontaneously.) combust. I look at Mrs. Foster and silently plead: *Give me a word already and put me out of my misery.*

Mrs. Foster clears her throat and motions toward my feet. I realize that her papers are scattered there. I gather them up and give them to her with trembling hands. I hear Mom's words again: *Still yourself, Vanessa. Still yourself!*

After adjusting her glasses and clearing her throat, Mrs. Foster says, "Your word is 'resuscitate.' "

I snort. I can't help it. I imagine a cute emergency tech resuscitating me on the floor of the stage. Unfortunately, when I snort, it makes a screeching noise in the microphone, and the people in the audience (even Mrs. Foster) cover their ears as though a supersonic jet has flown overhead. I see Mr. Martinez wince.

Why, I wonder, do I suffer such humiliation? What was God thinking when She made me?

Someone clears her throat. For a moment I think it's God, but then I look over and see Mrs. Foster tapping her watch.

My nostrils flare in a less-than-flattering way. I hate when someone taps a watch. I shake my head. *What is my word again? OHMYGOD!* I've completely forgotten. Sweat begins to pool under my arms. *Did I remember to apply deodorant this morning or did I just spray perfume and hope for the best?* "Could I have the origin of the word, please?"

"Resuscitate," Mrs. Foster snaps. "It comes from—"

"Resuscitate." I cut the principal off midsentence. "R-e-s-u-s-c-i-t-a-t-e. Resuscitate."

"That is correct." I imagine the "thank goodness and sit down" she doesn't say.

I curtsy—CURTSY? what am I, five years old?—then scamper back to polite applause. It's obvious I impress the audience by making it to my seat without tripping.

"Reginald Trumball, please come up."

Reginald turns and winks at me. At least I think it's at me. My heart goes into overdrive, and fingers of heat creep up my neck.

I notice my best friend, Emma Smith, staring at Reginald as he gets out of his seat. I wonder for a moment if she's even more in love with Reginald than I am. Not possible.

I watch Reginald jog to the microphone. He doesn't even stumble. That boy is all grace and good looks. If I'm lucky enough to have children with Reginald Trumball someday, I hope they inherit his good looks and quirky charm . . . and my ability to spell obscure (Obscure. O-B-S-C-U-R-E. Obscure.) words.

Mrs. Foster smiles and nods at Reginald. "Your word is 'categorize.' "

I close my eyes, squeeze my fingers into fists, and will the correct spelling into Reginald's gorgeous head. But something must be blocking my brain waves, because Reginald says: "C-a-t-i-g-o-r-i-z-e."

When the cowbell signals his defeat, Reginald's mother has her arm around his shoulders before he's even completely off the stage. Reginald puts his arm around his mother's shoulder and leans his head close to hers. She whispers something into his ear, probably about how he'll never need to spell that word again and how she'll take him out for ice cream later. I want that mother.

As I sit onstage gnawing on the skin beside my thumbnail, I wonder if my mom, the great Governor Rothrock, is even here today. I try to remember her schedule or if I even had breakfast with her this morning. I was so busy studying multisyllabic (Multisyllabic. M-U-L-T-I-S-Y-L-L-A-B-I-C. Multisyllabic.) words like, well, "multisyllabic" that my brain didn't have room for spare information like the presence of my mother or if I remembered to wear underpants this morning. I check discreetly. I did remember. The pair with purple hearts and red arrows. Whew!

Now, what was I checking for? Reginald's adorable face? No. Underwear? No. My mom? Yes! I strain from my seat and scan the crowd. Big hair. Toupee. Ugly bow tie. Twin women—how odd. Gray braid. Uni-brow. I search for

Mom's perfect coiffure. (Coiffure. C-O-I-F-F-U-R-E. Coiffure.) I look for the person who has played Scrabble with me since I was four, although we haven't played at all lately. And it's not because she's worried I'll win. I never have. Ever. Mom's that good. It's just that she's been a little, er, busy lately. And "busy" might be a slight understatement when describing my mom's daily schedule.

I spot Mom's press secretary, Mr. Adams, in the audience. He wiggles his fingers at me. I gasp and slink low in my seat. Mom sent her press secretary to watch me in the school spelling bee? Her *press secretary*! File *that* under neglect!

On the next round, I make it to the front of the stage without tripping or snorting into the microphone—hurrah—and spell "buoyed" correctly.

During each round, I watch chairs on the stage empty.

Unfortunately, during round six, Emma loses on the word "wildebeest." I told her she should have skipped a couple equestrian lessons to study more. She said she was a naturally good speller and didn't need to. After spelling "W-i-l-d-a-b-e-a-s-t," Emma is met with the harsh clang of the cowbell. Her shoulders sag, and she turns to me, blinking, like an injured deer. She tries to push the corners of her mouth up to show me she's okay, but she's sniffing and her shoulders are bobbing, and I can tell she's about to cry. I want to rush up and give her a hug, tell her there's always next year, but I'm not allowed to leave my seat. I hope she can read my thoughts. Emma shrugs, walks off the stage, and joins her mom in the audience.

I sigh and prepare myself for the next word, knowing I'll console Emma after the bee, during lunch.

Finally, it's between me and Darcy Clements. Darcy is a perfectly nice girl, except that she considers nose-picking a hobby. She and I go back and forth awhile. Darcy once told me she'd read every book in our school library. Slight exaggeration, I'm sure. Nonetheless, I sweat, pump my leg, and generally fall apart inside. On the outside, though, I'm like Merriam or Webster.

In the end, I whomp Darcy on the word "deficiency." I can't believe it. Such an easy word. Darcy left out the second *i*.

After I realize I won, I say, "Good job, Darcy," and she bursts into tears. I have no idea what to do. I pat her on the back, keeping far away from her pointer fingers—don't know where they've been lately—but she keeps sobbing. *Uh, a little help here, please.*

Suddenly, Darcy is gone and I'm engulfed by people saying "Congratulations" and slapping me on the back. Mr. Martinez moves in close. He doesn't like when people crowd me. It makes his job of keeping me safe harder. I'm afraid he'll tackle the principal, Mrs. Foster, when she drapes her arm over my shoulder and smiles for a photographer.

Emma is squished by the crowd but reaches her right arm toward me, wiggling her fingers. I stretch toward her hand, but our fingertips haven't quite touched when someone calls, "Vanessa. Over here." I turn, and a flash goes off.

Then another. I'm smiling and feeling pretty good until I get that pang, the one that feels like a big open space in the middle of my stomach. And I get that feeling because even though I'm surrounded by people, the one I need most in the world—my mom—isn't here.

After Mrs. Foster hands me a certificate with a gold seal and wishes me luck in the County Bee, I grab my backpack and head toward math class. Of course, Mr. Martinez follows a few feet behind. I'm still not used to being followed everywhere. I've had a bodyguard only since Mom won the Iowa caucuses about a week ago. Some kids think a pimple or a bad haircut makes them stand out. Imagine being trailed everywhere (and I do mean everywhere) by a six-foot-tall man wearing a dark suit and carrying a concealed weapon. As if I don't already have enough trouble blending in!

I squeeze my brows together, trying to remember where Mom is today. I know it's something important that I should remember, so I hit my forehead with the heel of my hand a few times to jar the information loose as I walk into Mr. Applebaum's classroom.

"You okay, Vanessa?" Mr. Applebaum asks.

"Yes," I sputter. "Just—a—a—mosquito."

"In January?"

"Uh-huh," I say, feeling heat creep up from my neck to the tips of my ears. I want to slink to my seat and do something constructive like, I don't know, die. Mr. Martinez waits outside the classroom as usual. The only thing more boring than sitting inside a seventh-grade math classroom has to be standing outside a seventh-grade math classroom waiting for the rare chance that something might happen. I mean, what could happen to me? Mr. Applebaum would hit me over the head with my math textbook? As if! That man's got to be the most harmless human being on the planet. New to Lawndale this year, he's the quintessential (Quintessential. Q-U-I-N-T-E-S-S-E-N-T-I-A-L. Quintessential.) nerd—complete with thick glasses and a pocket protector that holds his calculator.

I don't make it to my seat.

"Class," Mr. Applebaum says, his hand on my shoulder, "let's give Vanessa a round of applause. She and Reginald made it to the school bee. And Vanessa Rothrock, I was just informed"—he is beaming—"went all the way!"

OHMYGOD! Did my teacher just say that I, Vanessa Rothrock, age twelve and three-quarters, went all the way? I haven't even French-kissed a boy yet. To be perfectly honest, I haven't kissed a boy at all. Although as it turns out, the boy I'd most like to kiss in all of Lawndale Academy sits right next to me.

I slide into my seat and cannot even look at Reginald. I

feel like if I glance in his direction, my eyeballs will melt because I'm positive that boy can read my illicit thoughts about him.

Something pokes me in the arm. I brush it away. Another poke. I look over, totally annoyed to see Michael Dumas grinning. At least his eyelid isn't twitching. He gives me a double thumbs-up. What is he, Ebert *and* Roeper? I give him a weak smile and face front. Now I can't look right at Reginald or left at, ugh, Michael Dumas. I know it's a bad day when my best option is looking straight ahead at Mr. Applebaum, the only teacher in school who wears a bow tie—and that's his most attractive feature!

While he drones on and on about obscure geometric figures and their properties, I think of my winning word in the bee—"deficiency." I've certainly got several. Grandma says one can't improve until one recognizes one's weaknesses.

So, instead of paying attention to Mr. Applebaum, I do something constructive. I tear out a sheet of loose-leaf paper and list my deficiencies (D-E-F-I-C— Oh, whatever!) in purple ink. Later, I'll work on fixing the ones I can.

The Deficiencies of Vanessa Rothrock, Age 12¾

1. Boobs the size of cherry pits. (If life is a bowl of cherries, why are my boobs the pits?)

2. Mom is so busy I practically have to make an appointment to see her.

3. I'm probably the only girl in seventh grade who has NOT gotten her period.

4. I frequently embarrass myself by tripping over air molecules.

5. Did I mention how busy Mom is?

6. Feet so gigantic they could stamp out a forest fire—in the Sequoia National Forest, where Mom and Dad took me before—

When I hear Mr. Applebaum walk down the aisle, I throw my arm over my paper. *Please don't notice. Please keep walking.*

Mr. Applebaum stops. He taps my geometry book, looks over his glasses, and keeps walking.

"Thank God," I murmur.

"Excuse me," says Mr. Applebaum, turning back.

I want to bonk myself on the head. "Nothing."

"Okay, Vanessa. Pull it together, please. Open your book now."

I nod. I'm positive Reginald is staring at me, wondering why such a dweeb has to sit near him. I glance over. He's picking his teeth with his student I.D. badge. At least he cares about his dental hygiene.

I open my math book, turn to the page number written on the board, and stare at the image of a rhomboid. But I don't really see a rhomboid. Of course not. If I saw a rhomboid, I might be doing well in class. I see Reginald Trumball and me kissing in the Manatee Sculpture Garden at the Governor's Mansion.

"Ms. Rothrock!" says Mr. Applebaum.

OHMYGOD! Did I say something out loud? And how did Mr. Applebaum get to the front of the classroom without my noticing? I sit back in my chair and raise my eyebrows as if to say, "Who, me?"

Mr. Applebaum taps the board with his yardstick. "Please come to the board and draw a picture of a rhomboid for us."

I continue to stare.

"Any size at all is fine, Ms. Rothrock."

I gulp. There's no time to slip my list of deficiencies into my backpack or pocket, so I slide my textbook on top of it. As I walk down the aisle, I trip only slightly. This is a great improvement. I start to curtsy and stop myself immediately.

I squeeze the chalk, face the board, and write: "R-H-O-M-B-O-I-D."

The class laughs. Even Mr. Applebaum snickers. Don't they instruct teachers about protecting our fragile egos and self-worth by not laughing when we make complete idiots of ourselves, which I happen to do more often than most people?

"Uh, Ms. Rothrock," Mr. Applebaum says in a snide way, "maybe we could switch our brain from spelling mode to math mode."

Uh, Mr. Applebaum, maybe we can stop being so snide and sarcastic, I say in my head.

I draw a rhomboid that looks like a lopsided triangle on steroids. The class's continued laughter tells me three things.

Thing One: I have the artistic ability of a tree frog.

Thing Two: I did *not* draw a rhomboid.

Thing Three: The kids in this class are mean, except for Reginald, who is a god.

I look at Reginald to see how he's reacting to my utter humiliation. I am horrified to see that he's not reacting to anything I'm doing in front of the class. Reginald Trumball is leaning sideways toward my desk. More specifically, he's looking at the sheet of paper lying exposed on my desk. And here's the worst part: His lips are moving as though he's—gasp!—reading.

Even though Mr. Applebaum hasn't said I can, I march up the aisle to my seat and snatch the paper, crumple it, and shove it into my backpack. I face forward, absolutely certain I'm going to cry. The bell startles me. There is a God and She is good.

I wait until everyone else has left the classroom before I walk out. In the doorway, I see Reginald slam into Michael Dumas and I hear Reginald growl, "Watch where you're going, Dumb Ass!"

Reginald has been teasing Michael since fifth grade. Before that, they used to be best friends. Then Michael got glasses and a wicked twitch in his left eyelid. Meanwhile, Reginald got . . . gorgeous. *I should tell him to stop.*

Michael pushes his glasses up. "It's pronounced Doo-MAH, idiot! My name is Michael Doo-MAH!"

Go, *Michael!*

"Whatever, Dumb Ass!"

I cringe.

Mr. Martinez shakes his head at Reginald, and I watch Michael storm down the hallway. I feel the need to defend Reginald to Mr. Martinez, tell him Reginald's not usually like that. Tell him that he's cute and funny and that sometimes he winks at me.

I'm about to head toward the lunchroom to meet Emma, when Reginald moves closer to me. *Is this God's way of telling me I should say something to him about teasing Michael?*

Mr. Martinez steps toward me.

I hold up a hand.

Nodding, Mr. Martinez backs up.

"So, Vanessa," Reginald says, elbowing another boy in the ribs.

Is Reginald going to ask me out? My cheeks heat up. "Yes?"

"Vanessa," Reginald says, his friend nudging up against him, but looking at me. To be more specific, his friend is ogling my chest. Even though there is nothing of note to ogle, I casually pull my backpack in front of my chest. Reginald continues, "So, uh, Vanessa, how do you think you did on the, um, language arts test?" He eyes Mr. Martinez nervously, and I remind myself to beg Mom again about not having to be trailed by a security guard at school. If it makes Reginald Trumball nervous, it can't be a good thing.

What language arts test? "Um, okay, I think." Then I remember to consider others. And it's oh so easy to consider Reginald. I'm positive he'll grow out of his picking-on-

Michael phase. "How do you think *you* did on the, um, language arts test?"

Reginald elbows the boy next to him. "To tell you the truth, Vanessa"—he glances at Mr. Martinez, then whispers to me—"I think I did *the pits*. Get it? *The pits*."

As Reginald and the boy walk down the hall, I don't get it.

When they are far away, the other boy yells, "The pits!"

Then, suddenly . . . I get it!

I know Emma is waiting for me in the cafeteria, and I want to tell her that Reginald Trumball is a jerk, but I can't. What he did is too embarrassing. Instead of going to lunch, I run into the girls' bathroom and pick the stall farthest from the door. Mr. Martinez waits outside. I never get any privacy!

I wipe my eyes and nose with toilet paper. *How could Reginald read my list AND share it with some numbskull boy I don't even know? What is wrong with him? Doesn't he realize how much I—*

A sharp knock at the outer door. "You all right in there, Ms. Rothrock?"

OHMYGOD! "Fine." I sniff. "Be right out."

"No problem. I'm here if you need me."

Mr. Martinez's kindness makes me cry harder. *Why can't I cry in the bathroom stall during lunch like a normal girl? I* check my nose in the mirror. Red like the cover of my Scrabble dictionary. How embarrassing! I go back into the stall and tell myself to breathe deeply. But it doesn't smell so good, so breathing deeply isn't the best idea. *Did Reginald read my entire list? Oh God, please don't let him have read number three!* I should have told that boy he was a complete and total moron for making fun of Michael.

I take the crumpled list from my backpack and tear it into tiny pieces. I sprinkle the pieces into the toilet and flush twice to make sure they all go down. The last thing I need is the janitor reading my personal list of deficiencies, too.

When the bell rings, I decide I'm going to walk into class with my head held high, try not to trip, and get on with my day. That'll show Reginald I don't care a whit about him. *And I was having such a good day, with winning the spelling bee and all.* I rush out of the bathroom, past Mr. Martinez, and down the hall to language arts class. I hear Mr. Martinez's footsteps behind me.

When I see Reginald in class, I gasp, and a few kids look at me. *Do they know? Did Reginald share the items on my list with them, too?* I take my seat and copy the assignment from the board—write a poem about something about which you feel strongly. *Hmmm. I can think of one thing!*

How could Reginald have done something like that to me? He's never been mean to me before. I glance at the back of his head and shoot mental darts at it. *I hope you are run* over by a school bus today. Then I hope the driver realizes she forgot her double latte from Starbucks at school and drives the bus in reverse, running over you again. And one more time as she heads back out, her warm latte in hand.

This image makes me somewhat happier.

4

On the drive home, I spell words in my mind to relax. When we start up the driveway, though, my stomach seizes. *Will Mom be here?* If only I could remember where she is. I have so much to tell her. About winning the bee. About tripping at the bee. About what Evil Reginald did. Maybe I won't tell Mom about that. Or about tripping.

"Mom!" I run into the kitchen. "Mom!"

No answer.

Something on the counter stops me. Usually there is a plate of Mrs. Perez's lemon squares. Today, I stare at a huge bouquet of purple daisies. I inhale deeply but smell nothing and wonder stupidly if the flowers are an apology gift from Reginald. As if! I tear open the card.

Nessa,

You continue to make me proud. Congratulations on winning the school spelling bee.

Love and miss you,

Mom

I want to cry. Even though apology daisies from Reginald would have been nice, Mom scores definite points. I squeeze the card to my chest. Then I realize Mr. Adams probably ordered these the moment he left the bee today. He orders flowers or gift baskets for lots of people for Mom because she's too busy to do that kind of stuff. *Does Mom even know I won? And where is she?*

I leave the daisies in the kitchen and trudge up to my bedroom. I know I should be happy about winning the bee, but the boy I'm madly in love with crushed my heart today. And frankly, I wish Mom were here.

The Florida Room usually cheers me up—it's all windows and sun—but weekdays and Saturdays, I avoid it because it's a part of the mansion that's open to the public. As if I want to be sitting on the sofa looking out at the Manatee Sculpture Garden when some gawker comes in and takes my photo with his digital. I hang out there only on Sundays, when the mansion is all ours . . . and the staff's.

The thing I find funny about the Governor's Mansion is that the rooms have names. There's the Florida Room and the State Dining Room and the State Guest Room. Boring names, granted, but names nonetheless.

I didn't want my bedroom to feel left out, so when Mom won reelection, I celebrated by naming my bedroom. I call it the Purple Palace. I know it's totally weird to name one's bedroom, but I feel rather attached to it. It's full of my favorite color. And it's got all my stuff. My bedroom deserves a name. And naming my bedroom's not as strange as something I read once—that some guys name their weenies.

I drop my backpack on the Purple Palace's light purple carpet and plop down, leaning against my bed. Even though the room is full of things that usually make me happy—my purple-flowered comforter, my fuzzy purple lamp, seven (count them, seven) dictionaries (including the one Dad gave me that had sticky notes with arrows pointing to the words "I" and "love" and "you"—corny, but sweet)—nothing cheers me up today.

I'm not a naturally depressive person. Sometimes I can be downright exuberant. (Exuberant. E-X-U-B-E-R-A-N-T. Exuberant.) But today I'm not. And that's the fault of one mean and nasty boy—Reginald Trumball! Who does he think he is, reading my private, personal list of deficiencies? Just because I left it on my desk doesn't mean he had to push my math book off and read it. That boy clearly emerged from the shallow end of the gene pool.

Since I'm hopelessly depressed, I decide to study vocabulary for my usual two-hour session to get ready for the County Bee. Then I remind myself I won the school spelling bee today and can take one measly (Measly. M-E-A-S-L-Y. Measly.) day off. Of course, it's impossible to turn off my internal speller.

So, instead of pulling out my spelling notebooks, I grab a stack of letters from my desk. Fan letters. Like the kind famous people get, except they're for me because I'm the governor's daughter. I still can't believe strangers write to me. But every week, Mr. Adams's assistant delivers a stack she'd like me to answer. I'm supposed to read each letter, respond appropriately, and give the stack back. She reads my responses to make sure I don't write anything stupid— I don't—then mails them to the people who sent the letters.

The first letter is written in purple ink. My kind of kid.

Dear Vanessa,
   I hurd you like purpul.

I cringe at the misspellings.

   I think its so cool that you're Mom past a law to save the Everglades. Now allagaters and stuff can keep liveing. It would be sad if they dide. You're Mom must be a cool lady. You must be cool, to.
   Sinsirely,
   Todd Snider
   P.S. My teachur made me rite this.

I reply:

Dear Todd Snider,
　　Thank you for your letter. I'm glad you're happy about the new law to save the Everglades. The governor (a.k.a. my mom) worked very hard on that one. She's proud of it. And I'm proud of her.
　　Sincerely,
　　Vanessa Rothrock
　　P.S. My mom did not make me write this. ☺

After replying to all the letters, I remember I have homework. As if my hand isn't already about to fall off from answering fan mail. I look at the blank space in my planner next to "Math" and can't remember if we have homework because events during that class traumatized (Traumatized. T-R-A-U-M-A-T-I-Z-E-D. Traumatized.) me.

I wish Emma were in my math class so I could ask her about homework. I decide to take a break and call her anyway.

"Hi, Vanessa," she says, breathless.

"Hi, Em, what's up?" I bite the skin beside my thumbnail and think about whether or not I should tell her what Reginald did to me.

"I'm off to riding lessons," she says. "Mom's freaking out because I'm late. As usual. Can I call you later?"

"Sure."

"Okay. Talk to you soon. By the way, congrats on winning the bee."

My heart sinks. "Look, Emma, I meant to tell you how sorry I am that—"

"Don't worry, Vanessa. I'm so over it." She sniffs a couple of times. "Allergies."

"Yeah," I say, "there's a lot of pollen in the air." *There's no pollen in the air. It's January.* "Look, Em, 'wildebeest' is a dumb word. They tricked you."

"I know," Emma says. "Darcy Clements got words like 'pension' and 'trilogy' and I got 'wildebeest.' It's totally unfair."

I consider telling Emma about the mean thing Reginald did to me today, thinking it might make her feel better about losing the bee, but I can't make myself say the words. It's too humiliating to tell anyone, even Emma. "No, it's not fair. I wish there could be two winners from each school and you and I could go to the County Bee together."

"That would be cool," Emma says, "but I'm too busy with my riding. There's a big competition coming up. Anyway, you're the spelling champ at Lawndale, not me."

"Am not," I say, knowing that really I am. I spell words in my mind all the time. Sometimes even in my sleep!

"Yeah, you are. And this year, I have a feeling you'll go all the way."

I giggle. "I'm sure you didn't mean it like *that!*"

"Ohmygod! Shut up!"

We both laugh, but then her mom yells for her to hurry and she hangs up.

Not knowing what else to do, I pull out a sheet of paper

to work on my poem for language arts class. Mrs. Durlofsky said to write about strong feelings, so I think of writing about how Reginald made me feel today. But what Reginald did is entirely too personal to share with Mrs. Durlofsky. I consider writing about how I feel about Mom, but everyone already knows about her.

I come up with "Under the Microscope." It's not about science, though. It's about what it's like to be under public scrutiny (Scrutiny. S-C-R-U-T-I-N-Y. Scrutiny.) most of the time.

UNDER THE MICROSCOPE
By Vanessa Rothrock

I get letters, sometimes, from girls who say,
"I wish I were just like you."
But they don't really know what it's like
To be me, UNDER THE MICROSCOPE.
When I have a case of bed head, they're there
Snapping pictures for everyone to see.
When I trip or mess up, there is a microphone
Thrust in front of me.
No one would like that.
No one would want to be me . . . if they knew.
Even me. Sometimes.
I feel so out of place,
Like I'm such a disgrace
When I'm UNDER THE MICROSCOPE.

Someone knocks on my door. My heart leaps because I think it's Mom. I shove my poem into my backpack and hold my breath.

The door eases open and Mrs. Perez peeks in.

I let out my breath. Although I'm not happy to see Mrs. Perez, she seems ecstatic (Ecstatic. E-C-S-T-A-T-I-C. Ecstatic.) to see me. She swings the door wide open, and I hope the Purple Palace doesn't mind being so exposed.

"Vanessa," she says, beaming, "I'm so proud of you. I heard the good news about the spelling wasp. You won today at *la escuela*'s spelling wasp. No?"

"Yes, yes. It's called a spelling bee, though." I take Mrs. Perez's hand and it feels warm in mine. "That makes no sense, does it?"

Mrs. Perez shakes her head and laughs—a deep, hearty laugh. "Bee. Wasp. What's the difference? I'm sure my good speller is hungry, no? Dinner is ready." She turns to go, then whips back around. "Vanessa, did you see those beautiful flowers *de tu madre?*"

I nod less than enthusiastically.

"You no like them?"

"Oh, I like them." *They are purple*. "It's just that . . ."

"Ah," she says, putting an arm over my shoulders. "You miss *tu madre?*"

Mrs. Perez's warm body next to mine, her kind words . . . Instead of making me feel better, they make me feel like crying. But I must have used up my day's allotment (Allotment. A-L-L-O-T-M-E-N-T. Allotment.) in the girls' bathroom this afternoon, because not a single tear squeezes out.

When I'm finished with dinner—field greens salad, butternut squash soup, and flounder—and back in the Purple Palace, I wish I could crawl under my comforter and sleep through, I don't know, seventh grade. I don't want to face Reginald tomorrow. What if he laughs at me? Or worse, what if he told the whole school and *everyone* laughs at me? I pull the comforter over my head, and in the stifling darkness I remember something wonderful.

I leap out of bed and fall flat on my face. The comforter caught my size 9½ feet. Luckily, no one other than Carter, my stuffed toy donkey, is there to witness the embarrassing incident. I rub my nose and make it to the TV without sustaining further bodily injury. I flip on *Gilmore Girls* just in time to see Rory, the main character, have a heart-to-heart with her mother, and suddenly I get choked up. I realize I haven't heard from Mom at all today. I mean other than the cool purple daisies, which she may or may not have sent.

Right then, the phone rings. Mom and I are very in touch with each other, even when we're in different states. I just wish she hadn't called during our favorite show. Mom must be really busy not to realize what time it is.

I answer the phone. "Hey, Mom!"

"Excuse me?"

My mind races to place the voice that is making my heart slam against my chest. It's obvious my heart knows exactly who's on the other end of the phone, even if my brain doesn't. Then suddenly it does. I know who's on the phone. And I can't breathe.

5

"R-R-Reginald?" Oh, great. Now I'm stuttering! Let me add that to my list of deficiencies.

"Hey, Vanessa."

I hold the phone away from my ear like it's infested with fire ants. What do I say to the boy who totally humiliated me today?

"Vanessa? You there?"

His voice sounds soft and nice, but I shake my head and think of what he did today. "What?" I snap.

"Whoa. Look, Vanessa, I just called to—"

"To what, Reginald? To humiliate me again? Well, no thank you." I don't want anyone in the hall outside my room to hear me, so I lower my voice. "Once a day is quite enough. I can't believe you were so mean. What have I ever done to you?" *Other than love you?* I turn off the TV, gnaw on the skin beside my thumbnail, and press the phone to my ear. I can't believe those words just spewed (Spewed. S-P— Oh, for goodness' sake!) out of my mouth. I look over at Carter and am certain that were he a living donkey and not a stuffed toy, he'd be very proud of me.

Reginald sniffs. For a minute, I think he's crying. *Good.*

"I deserve that," he says.

You deserve a lot more than that!

"You still there? Vanessa?"

I hold my breath.

"I liked it better when you were yelling at me," he says.

I want to laugh, but hold it in. *Why does he have to be so cute?*

"I'm just calling to say, well, you know, that I'm . . . Vanessa, what I'm trying to say is . . ."

I know Reginald is suffering. But that's how I felt when I was crying in the girls' bathroom, so I say nothing to make this easier for him. He doesn't deserve my kindness, even though, for some stupid reason, I want to give it to him.

"Vanessa, I'm really, really sorry. What I did today was mean. And stupid. Jordan dared me. And it's just that—"

"It's okay." *Did I just say that?*

"No, Vanessa, it's not okay," Reginald says as though he's reading my mind. "I don't know what happens. Sometimes, when I'm around certain people, like Jordan, I act like an . . ."

I want to say "ass." I really want to say "ass." I really, really want to say "ass." I look at Carter, my stuffed, well, donkey, and remember that I, Vanessa Rothrock, am the governor's daughter. So, for Mom's sake, I hold it in.

"A complete idiot," Reginald finishes.

I bite so hard on the skin beside my thumbnail that the spot actually bleeds. I suck on it and taste metal. I want to hang on to my anger, but it's like squeezing a handful of sand—the harder I try, the more it slips away. "You didn't tell anyone else about my, um, list, did you?"

"Oh, no, Vanessa. I didn't. I swear. And I only told Jordan about number one. I'm really sorry. I totally understand if you hate me."

I let out a big breath. *Hate you? I've loved you since fourth grade when you punched Joey Simmons in the mouth for putting a live worm down my shirt.* "Just don't ever do anything like that again!" *How lame!*

"Believe me, I won't." Reginald says this in such a quiet, sexy way that I think I'll melt. "So, Vanessa, you finish that poem for language arts yet?"

I reach into my backpack and pull out my poem. "Yes. It's not good, but it's done. Did you finish yours?"

"Let me hear it."

"Huh?" My eyebrows shoot up. "Read? You? My poem?" I sound like I've been speaking English only a short time. "I told you. It's not good."

"Yeah, right," says Reginald. "Read it." The line is quiet.

I scan my poem. Not only isn't it good, it's actually bad. In fact, it's clearly abysmal. (Abysmal. A-B-Y-S-M-A-L. Abysmal.) "Oh, stop with the spelling already!"

"Huh?"

"Nothing. Sorry." I pound my forehead with the heel of

the hand that's holding the poem and poke myself in the eye with the corner of the paper. I blink incessantly while I read to Reginald. My eye waters so much it's hard to see the words. I worry that I'll lose vision in that eye. I can't lose vision because then I'll have trouble reading, get horrible migraines, and be unable to study for the county spelling bee. I'm so worried about losing my vision that I totally mess up my poem and have to read it a second time. As if reading it the first time wasn't embarrassing enough!

There is complete silence when I finish. I brace myself for Reginald's laughter.

"That's great, Vanessa. I mean it. That's a great poem. You are so talented."

Maybe, I think, *there's still a chance I will have Reginald's 2.3 children.* I swipe at my eye with my sleeve. The eye is still watering, but I'm pretty sure I can see.

"If you're not busy . . . ," Reginald says, and I immediately think he's talking about me having his 2.3 children. I blush fiercely. "Could you help me write mine?"

Gulp. "You want me to help you write your poem?"

"Well, yeah. You're good at writing and I'm . . . well, let's just say writing's not my best subject."

"What is?"

"Huh?"

I can't believe I just asked Reginald Trumball such a stupid question. I wish there were a rewind button on my mouth.

"Uh, I don't know. P.E., I guess."

"P.E. is cool," I say, not meaning it. I hate to sweat. I hate to wear the P.E. shorts and T-shirt because the shorts make my butt look too big and the T-shirt makes my boobs look too small (which they are). And Coach Conner is the meanest human being on the planet, outside of a few evil dictators who shall remain nameless. I guess I could learn to love P.E. if it means that much to Reginald. "What do you want your poem to be about?"

In the end, I write most of Reginald's poem—about winning a basketball game. By the time he says "Well, I'll see you in school tomorrow," I'm totally in love with him again. I mean, everyone makes mistakes.

I'm humming as I turn the TV back on. The credits for *Gilmore Girls* roll. *Why didn't I record it?* I realize Reginald and I were on the phone for nearly an hour.

I'm dying to tell somebody, but all I have available is Carter. "Nearly an hour!" I tell my stuffed donkey, shaking him as though it might activate his hearing. "Reginald Trumball spent nearly one hour talking with me on the phone." Carter appears nonplussed. (Nonplussed. N-O-N-P-L-U-S-S-E-D. Nonplussed.)

It doesn't matter, because my world is right again. There is still a chance with me and Reginald. And the first person I think of telling is Mom. But where is she?

When the phone rings again, my heart stampedes because I'm sure it's Reginald calling to ask me out. Could this day get any better?

I grab the phone. "Hey, Reginald," I say, trying to sound cool and calm even though inside I'm bursting.

"Reginald? Who's Reginald?"

My throat squeezes.

"Nessa, it's me. I don't have much time."

"Mom!" I turn off the TV and press the phone against my ear. I want to tell Mom everything about Reginald, at least the good parts. I want to tell her how he liked my poem and how we talked on the phone for nearly an hour. But all that comes out is "Where are you?"

"Excuse me?"

I'm not sure if Mom can't hear me or if I've put my size 9½ foot into my mouth by saying something stupid.

"Vanessa," she screeches. "Aren't you watching the news?"

As if I actually watch the news when she isn't here. "I was watching—" I start to say I was watching our show, *Gilmore Girls,* and I wish she'd been here to watch it with me. Then I realize I didn't watch it at all because I spent the time on the phone with Reginald. "Why?" I ask. "Did something happen?" I worry that Florida is about to be pounded by another hurricane and I was too busy on the phone with Reginald to hear about it, but this is ridiculous because hurricane season ended almost two months ago.

"Turn it on, honey. Turn on CNN."

I turn on CNN, and what I see knocks me backward. Fortunately, I fall on the most padded part of my anatomy. (Anatomy. A-N-A-T-O-M-Y. Anatomy.) *Oh, for goodness' sake!*

Mom's face takes up the whole screen. She's wearing the gold earrings Dad had given her when she first became governor. I'm used to seeing Mom on the local news, but CNN? That's for important people. I read the banner above Mom's head. "Ohmygod!"

"Nessa, you see it, don't you? Do you know what this might mean?"

I mumble the words on the screen: "Elyssa Rothrock, Governor of Florida, wins New Hampshire primary." My stomach drops as though I'd plunged down the tracks on a roller coaster without wearing a safety bar across my lap. *I know exactly what this might mean.* I thought when Mom won the Iowa caucuses last week, it was just a fluke and she'd lose the rest of the primaries, but this . . . This means she might actually have a chance to win her party's nomination. To run for president of the United States!

"That's right, Nessa. And with the Iowa caucuses win, this should give me the boost we need to take the lion's share of primaries in early February."

This is real.

"Isn't it wonderful?" she asked.

How did this happen? When Mom asked if I'd support her running for president, I said yes because I thought it would take her mind off things. I never imagined she actually had a shot at winning the party's nomination. I mean, Mom's got two things going against her—boobs! Didn't anyone bother to tell her she's a woman, and a woman has never been elected president of the United States, except on TV? I mean, she's a great governor. But president? She'll be so busy, I'll *never* see her!

"Nessa?"

"I'm here."

"What do you think?"

"About what?"

"Vanessa!"

I can't deal with this now. "Did you know I won the school spelling bee today? I'm going to the County Bee."

"Didn't you get the flowers I sent?"

I sigh. Mom did send the flowers. "They're beautiful. I totally love them. Purple is my favorite—"

"Coming, Arnie!"

I move the phone away from my ear. Arnie is Mom's campaign manager, and spends tons more time with her than I do. "Mom?"

"Looks like we're both winners today, Nessa!"

Then why do I feel like a loser?

"There's someone from National Public Radio waiting to interview me," Mom says. "I've got to go."

Trying to hold on to her a few moments longer, I whisper, "Love you."

"Coming, Arnie!" Mom shouts. "I've got to go. I'll call you tomorrow. Love you."

"I love you, too," I say to the dial tone.

As soon as I hang up, the phone rings. I'm hopeful it's Mom wanting to talk a little longer, but realize it must be Emma calling me back.

"Hey, Emma," I say.

"Emma? It's me, dear."

"Oh, hi, Grandma. Sorry, I thought you were—"

"Have you been watching the news?" Grandma says in a way-too-excited voice.

What is it with you Rothrock women? Of course I haven't been watching the news. I've been doing something much more important—talking to Reginald Trumball for nearly an hour! "Yes, of course I'm watching."

"Isn't it exciting?"

I let out a breath. "Yeah."

"Vanessa, you don't sound excited. What's wrong?"

"I'm fine, Grandma. Just tired. Did you know I won the school spelling bee today?"

"That's wonderful. Two Rothrock winners in one day."

"Thanks, Grandma."

"I've got to go tell my lady friends. I'm so excited."

I'm not sure if Grandma is talking about telling her lady friends about my spelling bee win or Mom's primary win, but I guess she's talking about Mom. "Okay, Grandma. Talk to you soon."

"Take care of yourself, dear. I'll see you soon."

"Okay. Bye."

After I hang up, I think of calling Emma. She's got to be done with riding lessons and homework by now. But when I start to dial her number, I realize I'm exhausted and don't feel like talking anymore.

I get into pajamas, grab Carter, and watch the news awhile to see Mom's face and hear her voice before I go to bed. I throw a kiss to the screen. "Good night, Mom."

7

When I wake, I enjoy fifteen blissful seconds before thoughts from last night rush into my mind and knot my stomach.

For the first time, there's an actual chance Mom will win her party's nomination (Nomination. N-O-M-I-N-A-T-I-O-N. Nomination.) to run for president of the United States. I might wake one morning, open my eyes, and be in a bedroom in the White House. I could sleep in the very room that Chelsea Clinton slept in. That would be cool because she and I have similar hair issues.

But then I remember something else—it's freezing in Washington, D.C., during the winter. And Grandma doesn't live in D.C.; she lives here in Florida in a fifty-five-and-older community where the ladies play bunco on Monday nights and pinochle on Wednesday nights and bingo on Friday nights if they're not taking a bus to the mall or the theater. She wouldn't give all that up to move with us. And worst of all, I probably wouldn't be allowed to paint my room even a very light shade of purple.

I squeeze my eyelids shut and push the thoughts from my mind. I've got to get ready for school.

I go into my bathroom and wish I could lock the door. A girl my age should be able to have complete and total privacy in that particular room. But I'm not allowed to lock a door. Ever. Security needs to be able to burst in and save me. What could they possibly save me from in my own bathroom? An alligator squeezing through the drain? As if! There was a tiny frog in the toilet once, but the only thing it did was make me scream. And then it made Mom and me laugh hysterically as Dad caught it in a shoe box and ran outside to the Manatee Sculpture Garden to set it free. It was hilarious at the time, but the memory makes me sad now.

I undress quickly and pull the shower curtain tight.

As the water runs down my back, I perform my morning ritual. I pull my elbows back and thrust my chest forward repeatedly while saying a prayer to the Boob Fairy. "If you're not too busy this week, Boob Fairy, please visit me. You've sprinkled magic boob dust on many of my classmates (most of whom are female), and I'm sure I must be next on your list. In case you've forgotten, I live at 700 North Adams. You'll recognize it because it's, well, the Governor's Mansion. And Florida is really nice to visit this time of year."

On the car ride to school, I pull a sheet of loose-leaf

paper and my purple pen with the feather from my backpack and write the following:

Reasons Mom Should NOT Run for President

1. I need her way more than the rest of the country does, even more than that guy with the hungry, cold family in New Hampshire I saw on TV last night. He said that Mom's his only chance to get back on his feet again. *Was he a plant?*

2. Mom will have to shake hands with a million people and might catch a horrible disease, like what happened to the president on that show *24*.

3. As if enough photographers don't already snap my picture when I look my absolute worst! Can't Mom wait to do this until after I'm out of my awkward stage, you know, like when I'm thirty?

4. And the most important reason Mom shouldn't run for president is: I don't want anything bad to happen to her.

I fold the paper and stuff it into my backpack. By the time the car pulls up in front of Lawndale Academy, my throat feels tight and tears are caught on my eyelashes. Why can't Mom be here with me, instead of off in some freezing state trying to convince people we don't know to vote for her so she can have a chance at a job I don't want her to have? I take a deep breath because, even though I miss Mom, I don't want to cry and make my nose all red and puffy for when I see Reginald.

When Mr. Martinez opens my door, Mrs. Foster's face is in front of mine. Her breath smells like peanut butter and coffee. *Hasn't that woman ever heard of Tom's of Maine or Mentos?*

"Come on, Vanessa," she says.

Mr. Martinez takes my arm and pulls me toward school. Mrs. Foster follows. I grip my backpack to me as though my life depends on it. *What's going on?*

"Vanessa! Over here."

I turn and a flash blinds me. Then more flashes. There is a tremendous crowd of reporters lining the path to school. For a moment, I think the reporters are there because I won the spelling bee. Then I realize all this fuss is about Mom's winning the New Hampshire primary. *Oh, why didn't I spend more time this morning on my hair and less time praying to the Boob Fairy?*

I imagine tomorrow's *Tallahassee Democrat* with a photo of me squinting and being dragged into school. Very attractive! I hope Reginald doesn't read the newspaper.

Why is this happening to me? How come I can't go to school like a normal kid and get picked on by bullies and stuff like that? A pox upon Mom's campaign! It's ruining my life.

Inside school, the quiet rings in my ears. I smile at Mr. Martinez, my way of telling him I'm glad he's here with me today. Big crowds give me the willies.

He winks. This makes me think of Reginald.

I remind myself to take deep, cleansing breaths as I walk

to my locker. By the time I get there, I'm hyperventilating. And what I see inside my locker doesn't help. On top of my math textbook is an envelope with my name on it. At first, I think someone in the school administration put it there. I mean, who else would have access to my locker? Then I notice a tiny heart on top of the *a* in my name. Mrs. Foster isn't the tiny-heart kind of principal.

I touch the envelope and realize it might contain a note from Reginald. But how could that boy have gotten it inside my locker without knowing the combination? I notice the slots in my locker door—they're just wide enough to accommodate (Accommodate. A-C-C-O-M-M-O-D-A-T-E. Accommodate.) an envelope.

I glance back at Mr. Martinez and shove the envelope into my backpack along with my textbooks and rush to class. I'll open it later when no one is looking.

In advisory with Mr. Applebaum, Reginald nods at me and winks as I approach. "Way cool about your mom," he says. "I saw her on the news last night."

Way cool? Did Reginald just say "way cool" to me? Maybe this campaign can be a good thing after all. "Thanks," I say. *Thanks? Is that the best I can come up with? Thanks? Way to show off your personality, wit, and large vocabulary, Vanessa. Now he'll never want to father your 2.3 children!*

I sink into my chair. I'm exhausted, and the day hasn't even started yet. I pull out the mystery envelope with the heart over the *a* in my name and feel energized. When I don't cut my finger sliding the flap open, I consider this a triumph.

Inside is a thick piece of cardboard with neat printing on it.

Dear Vanessa,
> **G.I. Haircuts**
> **G.I. Hats**
> **G.I. This**
> **G.I. That**
> **G.I. Like you**
> **G.I. Do**
> **G.I. Hope you like me, too.**

No signature. I glance at Reginald and he smiles at me, his wavy hair falling over one eye.

I tell my heart to slow down before Reginald hears it pounding. Maybe Reginald didn't really need me to help him with his poem last night. Perhaps it was just a ploy to keep me on the phone for nearly an hour. If this card is from him, it's obvious he writes perfectly good poetry. That boy is practically Shakespeare!

Mr. Applebaum grips my shoulder from behind. I gasp and slam my textbook closed over the card. *How did he get back there?* A creepy feeling washes over me. *Why must I have this man for both advisory AND math?*

Mr. Applebaum clears his throat and stands tall. I am looking up at the tiny hairs curling out of his nose. "Saw your mom on TV last night, Vanessa."

I wait for him to say something else. That he liked her.

That he didn't. He just stands there with his crooked bow tie and icky nose hair, blocking my view of something really important—Reginald, who would never allow hair to protrude (Protrude. P-R-O-T-R-U-D-E. Protrude.) below the level of his perfect nostrils.

After Mr. Applebaum walks to the front of the room, I rub my shoulder. He didn't have to squeeze it that tightly just because he saw Mom on TV. Big deal. My heart is still going crazy because of that poem someone—I glance at Reginald—dropped in my locker.

I'll never be able to focus on school today.

There is only one way to calm myself. I reach into my desk and pull out an old copy of *The American Heritage Dictionary*. I open to the *v*'s and start studying words because getting lost in spelling always relaxes me. I concentrate on the words in front of me, like "vacillate" (V-A-C-I-L-L-A-T-E) and "vacuity" (V-A-C-U-I-T-Y) and—OHMYGOD!—"vagina." I slam the dictionary shut.

I'm totally not relaxed!

When the bell rings, I rush straight to my locker. I check inside to see if the mystery admirer has deposited another envelope. I'm a little disappointed to find that other than some unimportant textbooks, my locker is completely empty.

"Hi, Vanessa."

I look up, hopeful. It's just Michael Dumas, waving as he walks past.

I give him a weak wave back, spot Emma, grab her

elbow, and walk her to her class. I whisper that I *have* to talk to her at lunch. Then I rush to social studies class because I'm late. Why do I have almost no classes with Emma Smith and tons with Michael Dumas? Were the people in scheduling trying to ruin my social life?

8

I can't wait to get to lunch and show Emma my mystery poem. But once I do, she insists on going up to Reginald to ask him if he dropped it in my locker. Instead of eating anything, I spend the entire period convincing her not to do that. It's Emma's fault I'm hungry and can't concentrate in language arts and mess up when I have to diagram a complex sentence at the board.

P.E. is no better. Coach Conner makes me run a mile. A mile! He is definitely a Republican. I can't help Mom's politics. Why should I suffer because of them? Of course, everyone in class has to run a mile.

But I'll bet no one else is thinking about the poem Reginald Trumball may or may not have dropped in her locker while running, er, in my case, taking a slow, pitiful jog that resembles dragging my legs as though they were sequoia tree trunks.

And I'll bet no one else is experiencing mondo cramps, either. I'm sure I'm a picture of grace and beauty dragging my tree-trunk legs and clutching my cramping stomach. What if . . . *OHMYGOD!* Here's something totally unfunny: What if I get my period right now? What if a giant red stain blossoms on the back of my white P.E. shorts while I'm dragging my pathetic excuse for a body around this track?

I'm not designed for physical exertion. Still, I'm ahead of Michael Dumas. Of course, he has asthma and has to walk. Lucky!

Something pokes me in the back. I swing at it. It pokes me again. I whirl around. It's Coach Conner. He's jogging beside me. Effortlessly. "Vanessa, when you finish this lap, get changed and head over to the office." *How can the man talk?*

"The . . . office?"

"Yes, they just called."

Who called? "Is . . . everything . . . okay?"

He shrugs and jogs off.

Give that man an F in compassion. I finish the lap as fast as I can, which is only slightly faster than a slug that just consumed its weight in Valium.

When I look in the locker room mirror, my face is so red it's purple, which is a really nice color, but not on my face! I'm not curious anymore about why I have to go to the office—I'm panicked. I don't bother to shower. I shove my sweaty clothes into my P.E. locker and yank on my regular clothes. I hobble out, my left foot only halfway in my boot. Soon I'm nearly running down the hall. And right before I get to the office door, I stop.

What if . . . Couldn't be. Not again. Still, I can't make my arm reach out and open the office door. As much as I don't want to know, I need to know. I take a deep breath and open the door.

Mrs. Foster turns to me, her lips parted. I'm sure bad news is about to spew from her mouth.

"Vanessa," she says, "what in the world happened to your face?"

Of course, I'm mentally spelling *s-p-e-w* as my fingers fly to my cheeks, which feel warm. I remember that my face is a bizarre shade of reddish purple from "running" in P.E. class. My utter embarrassment ratchets the color up another notch. "I was . . . running."

Her right eyebrow arches about two inches. *How does she do that?*

"Not in the halls," I say. I mean, I was . . . in P.E. I was—" *Ohmygod! Just tell me what happened to Mom!*

"Vanessa, relax." She pats my shoulder. "We called you to the office because your mother called."

I knew it! If my heart beats any harder, it will explode. *Tell me what she said! Is she okay?*

"Your mother said she wants you to leave school a little early today to avoid the reporters."

"That's it?"

Mrs. Foster looks at me like I'm crazy. "Well, yes,

Vanessa. What did you expect? A national parade in your honor?" She emits a fake laugh even though what she said was totally not funny. And I don't dare tell her what I expected. But she should know.

I leave the office, shaking my head. Why didn't Mr. Martinez just tell me we needed to leave early? When we emerge from the back door of the school, I'm surprised no reporters are there. Don't they know candidates and their families almost never use front doors? I breathe in cold air and am glad to be walking away from school.

With each block closer to home, a seed of hope sprouts. By the time we pull up in the driveway, it's blossomed into a wonderful thought. Maybe Mom called the school to have me leave early because she's home and wants to see me as soon as possible. Maybe when I walk into the mansion, she'll be there to greet me.

Mr. Martinez can barely keep up as I run up the driveway.

9

"Mom!" I drop my backpack on the kitchen floor and run so fast that when I make contact, Mom stumbles.

"Whoa, Nessa."

Hearing Mom say my name sounds so good.

Mrs. Perez busies herself in the kitchen squeezing lemons into a measuring cup, but I see her glance at us and smile.

Mom grips my shoulders and looks into my eyes, as though she hasn't looked into them for weeks. She hasn't. "Oh, Nessa," she says, her voice wobbling. A tear slides down Mom's cheek and smears through her makeup.

"Mom?" I'm afraid she's going to tell me some horrible news.

"I didn't know this would be so hard," she says, swiping at her wet cheek. "Being away from you. I know it's been only three weeks, but you look like you've grown."

I look at my chest. "Not here I haven't."

Mom laughs and gets spit on my face, but I don't wipe it away.

We hug for a long time. It feels so good I don't even tell Mom she's squeezing too hard. When she lets me up for air, Mom grabs one of Mrs. Perez's lemon squares. She closes her eyes after she takes a bite. "I've missed these. Remember when your father . . . ?" Mom shakes the unfinished thought from her head.

"Oh, Governor," says Mrs. Perez, "I'm making fresh ones. Wouldn't you like to wait for them?"

"No, Gloria, I'll just have another one when they're done."

This makes Mrs. Perez smile so wide her gold tooth shows. Mom has that effect on people.

"So, Nessa, tell me, have you been studying for the County Bee?"

I think of the poem dropped in my locker today. I think of Reginald being mean . . . then nice. I think of Coach Conner making me run a mile. *I've been entirely too busy to study.* Then I remember the three *v* words I looked at in the dictionary today. "Yes, I've been studying." *And if the word "vagina" is in the bee, Mom, I'll ace it.*

"Good to hear."

"Do you think you'll be able to come to the County Bee to watch me compete?" I say it casually, like I don't really care one way or the other, but inside my head, I'm thinking: *Please, please, please come.*

Mom pops the last bite of lemon square into her mouth and absently says, "I'll check with Arnie." She glances at her watch. "Can you believe it? Meeting in fifteen. I was hoping to have a little more time with you."

I deflate like a balloon. Mom's finally here, but she's not really here. "Do you have to go to the meeting?" I ask, hoping my pathetic look will sway her to cancel. "We could"— I take a deep breath—"play Scrabble."

Mom leans over and kisses my forehead. "I'd love to, Nessa, but I'm afraid you'll beat me."

"As if."

Mom ruffles my already ruffled hair and sighs. "Even if I'd like to pretend I'm not, I'm still the governor of Florida. And since I've been away campaigning, there are many things I need to take care of. Too many."

I notice dark circles under Mom's eyes and wonder if she has anemia. (Anemia. A-N-E-M-I-A. Anemia.) I remind myself to ask Mrs. Perez to ask the chef to fix Mom something with spinach for dinner.

"Nessa, do you know what tonight is?"

I'm afraid she'll tell me I have to attend a formal state dinner. I'm fully prepared to use studying for the bee as an excuse. "No."

"Well, I'm surprised. *Gilmore Girls* is on. And I want to make a date with you to watch it."

Campaigning has scrambled Mom's brain! "Mom, *Gilmore Girls* isn't on tonight."

"Yes, in fact, it is." She touches her index finger to the

tip of my nose. "I just hope you don't mind watching it again. I recorded last night's episode."

I perk up. And I don't tell Mom I never saw the show because of helping Reginald with his poem.

"I've scheduled one meeting after the next. But at eight-fifteen, I should be finished. So, let's meet in my bedroom at eight-thirty. You bring the popcorn."

Me, Mom, Gilmore Girls, *and a bowl of popcorn.* "That sounds sooo good." I kiss Mom on the cheek, grab a lemon square, and run up to the Purple Palace.

10

I make the unusual decision to skip my prayers to the Boob Fairy so I'll have maximum time with Mom before school. I hope she appreciates my sacrifice. I mean, now that Reginald may be my secret admirer, it's more important than ever that my uncooperative boobs get with the program.

My wet hair slaps my neck as I rush to the kitchen, expecting to see Mom reading her stack of newspapers with her mug of coffee, bowl of grits, and overripe banana nearby.

But when I walk into the kitchen, all I actually see are the following: a bowl of cereal at my place at the table, a glass of orange juice, and an envelope with my name on it. Block letters. No heart over the *a*.

Dear Nessa,

I'm so sorry we didn't have more time together. I apologize for falling asleep last night during our show. I was exhausted. This campaign schedule is killing me.

Poor word choice, Mom.

I had to catch a night flight to attend an early-morning rally. Interviews and meet and greets the rest of the day. I'll call soon.
Love,
Mom

There's still nearly half an hour before I need to leave for school. Time I'd hoped to spend with Mom. *Did Chelsea Clinton feel like this when her dad was running for president? Of course not. She still had her mom at home. I don't have either.*

Without touching breakfast, I drag myself into the family room, flip on CNN, and perform half-hearted chest-enhancing exercises while hoping to get a glimpse of Mom. Other kids don't have to watch TV to see their moms before school. When I hear Mom's name, I turn up the sound and focus on the screen.

"When Governor Elyssa Rothrock appeared before a crowd early this morning . . ."

Mom's on a small stage, gripping a railing and waving at people who are holding signs and cheering. She pumps her fist in the air and then, suddenly, she's not on the stage anymore.

My hands fly to my mouth.

11

"Ohmygod!"

Mrs. Perez runs in, wiping her hands on a kitchen towel. She kneels in front of the TV. "Vanessa. *¿Que? ¿Que? ¿Es tu madre?*"

My fist is in my mouth. I shake the remote at the TV and hit "rewind" on the TiVo. Even though I know exactly what's going to happen because I just watched it, when the stage's railing gives way and Mom tumbles to the ground and a pile of people land on top of her, I scream again.

"*¡Ay, Dios mio!*"

I follow Mrs. Perez to the press secretary's office. "Mr. Adams," Mrs. Perez says, breathless, "if you please, what has happened to—?"

Mr. Adams is on the phone. He waves at Mrs. Perez to be quiet.

I'm so glad Mrs. Perez is squeezing my shoulders because

if she lets go, I'll fall to pieces. *Is Mom okay? Did she break something? What if she broke her neck? Could she be . . . dead? For God's sake, Mr. Adams, hang up!*

He does, and looks directly at me. "Vanessa, your mother is okay."

My knees give out, and Mrs. Perez tightens her grip, holding me upright. She whispers in my ear. *"Tu madre esta bien. Bien."* Then she squeezes my shoulders so hard it actually hurts, but I don't mind.

Mr. Adams continues: "A railing gave way on a stage where your mother was speaking. It wasn't constructed properly. She's bruised, but I promise you, Vanessa, she's okay."

I gulp. "I need to talk to her."

He shakes his head. "Sorry, Vanessa. She's extremely busy. I couldn't even talk to her. Arnie passed along the news. But there's no need to worry."

No need to worry! I shake free from Mrs. Perez and run up to my room. I climb in bed, pull the comforter over my head, and hug Carter to my neck.

Someone knocks at my door. I pull the comforter off my head and hear Mrs. Perez's labored breathing before she even opens the door. When she does, she looks sad. "Vanessa, please don't worry. Your mother *esta bien. Bien*, and that is *bueno*."

"Thank you, Mrs. Perez, but I need to be alone."

She nods and closes the door.

I pull the comforter over my head again. *How could this*

have happened? Aren't there people there to protect her? How do I know Mom's really okay? How dare Mr. Adams tell me I can't talk to my own mother?

I scramble out of bed and grab my phone. *Only in an emergency,* I hear Mom's words in my head. This is an emergency!

"Arnie here."

"Arnie, how is—?"

"Vanessa, sweetheart. Your mom was afraid you'd see the news. She hasn't had a moment to call. You've seen it, haven't you?"

I nod as though he can see me. "Yes," I peep, now imagining Mom in traction in the hospital.

"Your mom's okay, Vanessa. I promise."

I nod again. "May I please talk to her?"

There is silence, and I'm sure he's figuring out how to get rid of me without letting me talk to Mom. I'm ready to call Grandma and tell her we've got to get on a plane to make sure Mom's really okay, even though the last thing I want to do is get on a plane.

"Nessa?"

Relief washes over me and I bite my bottom lip to keep from crying. "Yes?"

"You didn't have to call, honey. I'm fine. Honestly. I'll have a nasty bruise on my shoulder, but I've had X-rays and—"

"X-rays!"

"Of course. They had to make sure nothing was broken.

You can be sure I'll check railings from now on. That really startled me. And the police. They were so sweet. 'How do you feel, Governor Rothrock?' 'Can we get you anything, Governor Rothrock?' One of them gave me his coat while I waited for the ambulance."

"Ambulance? Mom!"

"Just a precaution. I'm telling you, Nessa. I'm one hundred percent fine. In fact, I'm late for an interview. This fiasco has set me behind, not to mention made me look like a buffoon. I'm sure the opposition is going to have a field day with this one. If they're smart, though, they'll leave it alone."

I'm spelling "buffoon" in my mind, so I know I'm okay.

"Nessa, I've got to get back to work."

When Mom doesn't say anything for a moment, I'm afraid the doctors missed a concussion and her brain isn't operating at full capacity.

"And you need to get to school. Now."

Her brain's fine.

"Please, sweetheart, don't worry about me."

Don't worry about you? That's like telling me not to trip.
"Mom?"

"Yes, Nessa?"

"I love you."

"Oh, honey, I love you, too. Now, get to school before you're late."

On the ride to school, I play the news clip over and over in my mind. What if Mom wasn't okay? What if something worse than a railing falling had happened? What if . . . ?

When the car stops, I see reporters near the school's rear entrance. I reach for the door handle, then remember the rule: Never get out of the car when it stops. That is the time you are most vulnerable. Wait until the area is secured. Someone will open the door and get you out.

And that's exactly what happens. Mr. Martinez opens my door and offers me his hand. Such a gentleman. Then he yanks me out and rushes me to school. Reporters call my name and snap photos.

I can't put up with this for ten more months. Maybe the voters won't like that Mom fell and will stop voting for her in the primaries. Then life can get back to normal. This thought makes me smile, and as I do, someone snaps my photo. *Finally, a photo where I look happy.*

Inside school, I open my locker and am shocked to see another envelope with a heart over the *a* in my name. Because of Mom's accident this morning, I'd completely forgotten about having a secret admirer. But apparently my secret admirer hasn't forgotten about me. I shove the envelope into my backpack, feeling better than I have all morning.

Fortunately, during advisory, Mr. Applebaum is furiously writing something at his desk, completely oblivious to the class, so I have plenty of time to open my envelope and linger over the card inside.

Vanessa,
How do I like thee? Let me count the ways.
1. You're funny.
2. You're smart.
3. You're not bad at art.

Yes, I am. Once I drew a picture of a penguin and Mom said it was an excellent rendering of a Dalmatian.

4. You're great at smelling, oops, selling, um, spelling.
5. Your eyes are fine.

I notice "fine boobs" is nowhere on the list. Whatever!

6. The purple clothes you wear are divine.

Very funny.

7. I'd like to hold your hand in mine.

OHMYGOD!

I glance at Reginald and blush fiercely. *He wants to hold my hand?* Reginald pretends to do homework at his desk. He's probably too embarrassed to look at me. I had no idea he could write poetry like this. The only time I heard Mrs. Durlofsky compliment his poetry was after I helped him write the one about winning a basketball game. That boy's got more depth to his soul than I ever imagined.

I reread the poem throughout advisory. My cheeks get warm every time. But by the middle of first period, the glow of the card has worn off and I'm worried about Mom again. Maybe her fall was God's way of telling her to drop out of the race. She should listen to God. What if something worse happens? She should stop this campaign stuff and come home. Why does she need a whole country to run? I've got enough going on in my pathetic life to keep her busy for at least the next four years!

I tap my pencil eraser against my lips. Maybe, if I were lucky enough to contract some horrid disease, Mom would drop out of the campaign to take care of me. Nothing too ghastly, of course, because I'm not good at dealing with pain or swallowing pills.

I think of the medical terms I've been studying for the bee. Maybe a simple case of hypothermia (Hypothermia. H-Y-P-O-T-H-E-R-M-I-A. Hypothermia.) would do the trick. I snort. As if I could actually be stricken with hypothermia in Florida!

I spend the rest of the day alternating between obsessing about my secret admirer and coming up with a disease I could get that's bad enough to make Mom stop campaigning but not bad enough to kill me. There's got to be something. Maybe impetigo. (Impetigo. I-M-P-E-T-I-G-O. Impetigo.) I'd have unsightly skin lesions and be highly contagious. Mom could catch it . . . if she was ever home long enough to catch it.

But as much as I want Mom home with me, I know this campaign means the world to her. She's told me the story of Victoria Woodhull a dozen times. Woodhull was the first woman to run for president of the United States, fifty years before women were even allowed to vote! How cool is that? Obviously, she didn't win. But when Mom was ten and read a book about Victoria Woodhull, she decided she wanted to be president. That's a long time to know what you want. The only things I've wanted since I was ten are boobs.

Who am I to stand in the way of Mom's lifelong dream?

13

Coach Conner barking instructions in P.E. snaps me back to reality, and I don't like what I see.

The horse is set up in the middle of the gymnasium with thick blue mats beneath it.

Not a real horse. The kind with two handles on top that I'm supposed to grab as I leap over. As if! I have enough trouble leaping over carpet fibers and dust particles without tripping and falling flat on my face. *Not everyone is on steroids, you know, Coach Conner!*

There are two people in front of me before it's my turn to run and jump over the ridiculously high apparatus.

I groan my disappointment when Josh Friedman runs, leaps, and easily clears the horse. *I hope those mats are soft.* The next person, the one who will jump before me, is Michael Dumas. And unless he takes forty minutes to run and jump, I'll be forced to take my turn. It's not that I don't like Michael, but right now, I hope he stumbles and breaks the horse so badly we'll be forced to switch to badminton.

OHMYGOD! Michael Dumas's skinny legs don't even touch the horse as he leaps over to the other side. *Thanks a lot, Michael!*

Since Michael is on the other side, there's nobody standing between me and that horse. Even Mr. Martinez is stationed by the far wall, not doing a single thing to protect me from the upcoming humiliation.

"Run and jump over that horse!" Coach Conner barks.

What if I get hurt? Look what happened to Mom this morning. I could seriously injure myself. Then Mom will have to take time off from the campaign and—

"Run, Rothrock!"

I charge toward the horse, grab the handles, and stop.

"Rothrock!" Coach Conner shouts, coming closer and slapping his clipboard. I see Mr. Martinez take a step toward us, and am grateful. I wonder if Mr. Martinez could take Coach Conner. Coach is pretty muscular. But Mr. Martinez probably knows martial arts and stuff. Besides, he's got one thing Coach Conner doesn't have: a gun.

"Rothrock?"

The class's laughter tells me three things:

1. Coach Conner has been talking and I haven't been listening.

2. I'm making a complete idiot of myself in front of the entire class.

3. P.E. should be illegal in Florida, if not in all fifty states and Samoa.

"Can we try that again?" Coach Conner asks, looking directly at me. Then his voice escalates. "And this time actually jump *over* the horse!"

I'm not sure whose face is redder—his or mine. Kids laugh behind me. I glance at the clock near Mr. Martinez and will time to magically shoot forward so that this torture will end and I can go home to the Purple Palace and a nice warm lemon square. I can almost taste sour lemon on my tongue·when—

"Rothrock!" Coach Conner drums his fat fingers on his clipboard and says, in a singsong voice, "Can we do this before, oh, I don't know, Election Day?"

Election Day? My stomach tightens. *What do you mean by that, you Neanderthal? Wait. You're not a Neanderthal. You're a . . . you're a . . . Republican. I knew it! That's what this is all about.* I grind my heels into the mat. I look at the horse. *It's not so high. I can do it. This is for you, Mom.*

I run forward, feet pounding, arms pumping. I see Michael on the other side of the horse. Since he went before me, he's my spotter. His arms are extended and his eyes are hopeful.

If I hurt myself, Mom will have to take time off from the campaign—

I grab the handles, lean my weight on my right arm,

and sail upward, throwing my legs over the left side. *I'm doing it!*

My size gigantic foot catches on the end of the horse and I tumble forward. Fortunately, my head breaks my fall. Actually, my left arm breaks my fall. And when it does, I hear a loud snap. Pain shoots from my wrist. "Aaaah!"

Michael stares at me, his arms still outstretched as if to catch me.

I look down, tears welling in my eyes. I am a puddle of pain and humiliation.

"Good thing the mat was there, huh, Rothrock?" Coach Conner laughs. "You're okay, right?"

I look up and grimace, afraid to jar my arm. I can't stop tears from flowing; I've never felt physical pain like this before.

Michael Dumas kneels before me and touches my left hand so gently it feels like a butterfly landed. I look into Michael's eyes, and for the first time since kindergarten, I notice they're a gorgeous shade of green, like the emerald in Grandma's favorite necklace.

Michael steps back, and Coach Conner grabs my left arm above the elbow and shakes it as though he's trying to dislodge my hand from my wrist. "Arm okay, right, Rothrock? Just shake it out."

"Aaaargh!" Tears stream down my cheeks. I see flashes of light and feel like I'm going to faint.

"Stop!" Michael screams. "You're hurting her."

I see panic in Coach's eyes. "Your arm's okay, right, Rothrock?"

My arm is definitely not okay, you . . . you . . . you Republican!

Mr. Martinez charges forward and knocks Coach Conner away from me. Kids gasp. Coach lies on the mat, stunned and red-faced.

Mr. Martinez gently puts his arm around my shoulders and whispers, "Can you stand?"

I nod, shaking tears onto the mat.

"Okay, we're going to stand," Mr. Martinez says. "Slowly."

I do and my wrist explodes with pain. I can't believe anything can hurt so much. I'm panicked that the thing poking from beneath my red, swollen skin is my bone.

As Mr. Martinez and I walk toward the door, I look back and see Coach Conner stumble to his feet. Most of the kids stare in my direction. In the quiet of the gym, I hear a basketball bouncing on the wood floor. Reginald Trumball, love of my pathetic life, is at the far end of the gym shooting baskets while I'm cradling what is sure to be a broken wrist.

"Good luck, Vanessa."

I turn toward the voice. Michael Dumas waves with one hand, the other pressed to his mouth.

14

The eight most horrible things about being in the emergency room:

1. I'm still wearing my embarrassing P.E. T-shirt and shorts. As bad as they are, they're preferable to the peekaboo-view hospital gown a male nurse offered me. As if!

2. My wrist really hurts.

3. It smells like alcohol in here—the kind rubbed on your skin before you get a needle. And even though I hate getting needles, that would be way less painful than how my wrist feels.

4. Did I mention how much my wrist hurts?

5. Even though the administrator of the hospital came to see me, no one gave me anything for pain until Mom could be reached. And that took nearly forty-five minutes.

She was meeting with the mayor of Cincinnati or something. File *that* under neglect!

6. Even with pain medicine, my wrist still hurts.

7. Some inebriated (Inebriated. I-N-E-B-R-I-A-T-E-D. Inebriated.) guy on a gurney just rolled by. He smelled like alcohol, but not the stick-a-needle-in-your-arm variety. He was singing "Can you tell me how to get, how to get to Sesame Street?" and his hospital gown flopped open. Mr. Martinez shut the curtain around my bed in a big hurry, but not before I got a full view of the guy's hairy you-know-what!

But the most horrible thing about being in the emergency room is . . .

8. I'm completely surrounded by people, but not one of them is my mom.

"She's on her way," Mr. Adams assures me. Then he mutters, "This has certainly been a day for accidents."

Grandma looks positively pale as the orthopedist sets my bone. I scream. It hurts worse than breaking it in the first place. He slips a cotton glove with the fingers cut off on my hand and positions my fingers downward. While he takes a fiberglass cast out of a plastic bag and runs it under water before putting it on, I keep expecting to see Mom walk in, but she never does.

There's one positive thing, though. I get to choose the

color of my cast: blue, green, pink, or purple. I choose purple. It will match all my clothes.

Back home, Grandma piles pillows for me to rest my broken wrist on. I have to elevate it above my heart. My hand is swelling and I'm afraid the cast is going to explode. I try to wiggle my fingers, but they're fat and stiff.

Mrs. Perez brings me a tray with a flexible ice pack to wrap around my cast, a bowl of chicken soup, and a warm lemon square. I'm starving, but I feel nauseated. Probably from taking pain pills on an empty stomach. I manage a few sips of soup, glad I didn't break my right arm. How would I eat? Write? Study?

Study! I need to focus on studying for the County Bee. OHMYGOD! How am I going to concentrate with this thing on my arm for eight to ten weeks? My panic subsides slightly when I realize I learned some new spelling words today:

1. R-A-D-I-U-S—the bone I broke on the far side of my wrist.

2. E-D-E-M-A—a fancy word for swelling, which my arm is doing like crazy underneath my cast.

3. I-N-E-B-R-I-A-T-E-D—the guy who rolled by on the gurney.

Mrs. Perez stands, wringing her hands, while Grandma sits on the edge of my bed. "Can I get you anything, dear?" Grandma asks. "More pillows? Is the pain medication working? Do you need—"

My door bursts open.

"Nessa!"

I'm so startled I upend the tray with my good arm. Warm soup soaks through my pajama bottoms. *Could this day get any worse?*

I'm prepared to be angry with Mom. *How could she have been unavailable when I needed her most?*

But the instant Mom gasps at my cast, rushes over, and kisses my forehead, I'm toast. All I want is to be alone with her. I'm sorry it took breaking my wrist to get her back, but I'm glad she's here.

Both Mrs. Perez and Grandma wipe at my pajama bottoms with tissues. So, instead of chicken-soup-soaked pajamas, I have chicken-soup-soaked pajamas with bits of blue tissue stuck to them. I look at Mom, pleading with my eyes.

Mom kisses Grandma on the cheek. "Thanks, Mom. You were a lifesaver today." Then she looks at Mrs. Perez. "Gloria, I really appreciate all you did today, but I'll take it from here."

Mrs. Perez gives a little nod, grabs the tray, and leaves.

Grandma kisses my forehead, looks at me with pity, and says to Mom, "I'll call you, Elyssa." From the doorway, she throws me a kiss. "Elevate, dear. Elevate."

If I raise my arm any higher, every teacher within a three-mile radius will call on me.

As soon as my bedroom door closes and I'm alone with Mom, I weep. I weep because my wrist is swollen and painful. I weep because my pajamas are soaked with chicken soup. But mostly I weep because Mom is finally here.

"Pain?" Mom asks.

I nod because I can't explain all my feelings. Mom hands me tissues and lets me cry until I can't anymore.

"Better?"

I nod. "Except that I smell like a bowl of chicken soup."

Mom and I both laugh.

"Let's get you cleaned up," she says. "Can you walk?"

"I broke my radius, not my femur," I say, attempting humor. But the minute I move my arm, pain blindsides me and I don't feel the least bit funny.

"Let me get you a pill," Mom says.

I close my eyes and nod. "Bathroom. Medicine cabinet." I'm already sick to my stomach, and don't want to take another pill without eating something, so I take a bite of the lemon square.

Mom returns with a pill in her palm. One dry pill. *Doesn't she remember I hate taking pills? That she used to put medicine in a bowl of applesauce for me when I was younger? It took a dozen gulps of ginger ale for me to swallow the pill in the hospital, and even then it got stuck.*

I think of how much I needed Mom today when she wasn't there. Anger bubbles inside me and I blurt, "Where were you today?"

"Oh, Nessa." She smooths my unsmoothable hair. "You know I was campaigning and—"

"You should have—" I choke on a bit of sour lemon square. I'm coughing, but want to tell Mom I was scared when I heard my wrist snap. I think of the smells and sights in the emergency room. "You should have been with me. I needed you, and you weren't there." I realize I sound whiny, but don't care.

Mom takes a deep breath. "Vanessa, please take this pill. The pain is probably getting to you." She grips the elbow of my good arm. "And we'll—"

I jerk away from her, accidentally knocking the pill out of her hand and banging the back of my head on the headboard. "Just go," I say, rubbing my head. When my throat gets tight and tears gather on my lower lids, I turn my head away.

"Vanessa, I can't help you if—"

"Don't," I say. My skin is wet and cold, and I know I'm going to start sobbing any minute. "I don't want your help."

"Vanessa, at least turn around and look at me."

I refuse to turn my head, not to be defiant, but because I don't want to cry in front of Mom right now.

"I flew all the way back here so that I could . . . Oh, never mind!"

I hear my bedroom door slam. And my tears begin to flow.

Changing out of soaked pajamas while wearing a cast is almost as challenging as replacing chicken-soup-splattered sheets with fresh ones while wearing a cast. As soon as I secure one corner of the sheet, the other pops off. And it's especially daunting because every movement sends pain shooting through my arm.

By the time I climb back into bed in dry pajamas, I'm so exhausted that I elevate my arm and immediately fall asleep.

A couple of hours later, I bolt awake, spelling "assassination."

My dream was horrible. I was onstage at the bee, but it wasn't the bee. It was Mr. Applebaum's classroom and everybody was there—Reginald, Michael Dumas, Mr. Martinez, Coach Conner, Grandma, and Daddy.

Acting like a robot, Mr. Applebaum said, "Vanessa, your word is 'assassination.'"

In my dream, I knew something was wrong, but I couldn't figure out what it was. I'd gotten up to "A-s-s" when I searched the audience for Mom and realized she wasn't there. I panicked and messed up my word, saying nonsense letters like "m-n-o-p" and "x-y-z" and "t-t-f-n."

Just then, a masculine-looking woman started laughing. She raised her arm, which had a cast on it, and pointed a gun . . . at me!

I heard Mom scream, "I'm here, baby!"

Then, in my dream, I looked down and saw that I was totally and completely naked, except for a pair of blue bedroom slippers that looked like Carter.

OHMYGOD! I even embarrass myself in my dreams!

Just to be sure now, I look down. I'm wearing pajamas—the ones I changed into before bed. I can't wiggle the fingers protruding (Protruding. P-R-O-T-R— Ah, it hurts!) from my cast because of the swelling. My wrist is throbbing. And I'm hungry and sick to my stomach at the same time.

I ease out of bed and walk down the hall to Mom's room, nodding at the security guard posted by her door.

I knock quietly. No answer. I ease the door open and see Mom at her desk wearing her silky, sleeveless nightgown. "Hi," I say.

Mom whips around. "Oh, Nessa. You startled me."

I can't tell if she's still mad about how I acted before. "I can't sleep," I peep from the doorway.

"Come over here," Mom says, opening her arms.

Not mad. I go in and shut the door behind me. "Mom, I'm really sorry about—"

"Don't." Mom holds up a hand. She gets up and takes me over to sit on the edge of the bed, and she sits next to me. "You were right, Nessa. In a way. I've got to be more attentive to your needs. I must focus more on parenting." Mom sighs. "Campaigning is so demanding. And with so many important primaries in just a few days . . . The truth is, I haven't figured out how to do both things well."

Don't do both things.

"At least you're okay now." She pats my knee.

I hold up my cast. "Actually, this is killing me."

She tips her forehead against mine. "I'm sorry." When she pulls back, I notice dark, puffy bags under her eyes.

"Have you slept?" I ask.

She nods toward the piles of paper on her desk. "Can't."

"Me either."

Mom ruffles my already wild hair. "I have an idea."

As Mom walks toward her closet, I notice a huge purple-black bruise blossoming around her shoulder. I gasp, remembering when she fell off the stage earlier today.

Mom turns with a box in her hands. "Scrabble?"

Mom, please be okay. "Now?"

She shrugs, and I wonder if it hurts her shoulder.

"Can you think of a better time for me to beat you?"

"We'll see about that," I say, taking the box from her.

16

These are the things I learn about playing Scrabble with Mom at one in the morning:

1. No one calls and interrupts us, which is really nice.

2. We giggle about silly things, like the word "qwerty" in the Scrabble dictionary.

3. My wrist doesn't hurt so much when I'm focusing on a way to combine an "x" and a "j" in one word. As if!

4. It's impossible to avoid bumping the board when you're wearing a bulky purple cast.

5. Even though Mom is so tired she's slurring her spoken words, she manages to beat me by eighty-one points.

"You're slipping," I tell her as I put away the tiles.

"I'm just tired," she says, and winks. "I'll beat you by more next time."

"Promises, promises," I say as I leave her room.

While lying in bed, I turn her words over in my mind: *next time*.

I wake to throbbing pain in my wrist and a faint smell of chicken soup in my bed. My fingers are so swollen I still can't bend them. The thought of taking a shower while keeping my cast dry is too daunting (Daunting. D-A-U-N-T-I-N-G. Daunting.) for a Saturday morning, so I head downstairs instead.

I stop before the landing. *Was she even going to tell me?*

Mom is standing at the door with her driver, who is holding Mom's suitcase and garment bag. Grandma stands nearby with two of her own suitcases and a bag from Publix at her feet. *Two suitcases! How long is she staying? Mom must have called her last night. Couldn't she have told me?*

"Nessa!" Mom says, opening her arms.

I don't move.

"I was just going to send someone to wake you. Come on down, now. Give me a hug." She looks at her watch. "I must get going."

I feel my body deflate like a tire gone flat. I trudge down the stairs and allow Mom to kiss my forehead.

"How's your wrist?" she asks.

"Still sore," I say, but Mom's already turned to give instructions to her driver.

"Hello, dear," Grandma says, giving me a peck on the cheek. "Wait till you see what I've got in the bag."

I look at Mom. *Don't go. I don't want Grandma, I want you.* My wrist throbs.

Mom bends and whispers in my ear. "Grandma's just moving in for a while to keep an eye on you." She nods toward my cast.

Moving in? I step closer to Mom, remembering something. "When are you coming home?"

She touches the side of my face. "Oh, Nessa. You'll be okay."

"Mom, I need to know. When?"

She looks out the door at the waiting car.

"Will you be able to watch me at the County Bee?" I ask.

Mom takes my chin in her fingers. "Nessa, I'll be there, unless—"

"Unless *what?*" I practically shriek.

Grandma examines her nails as if nothing is going on right next to her. I love Grandma, but I wish she weren't here right now.

Mom shakes her head. "Unless nothing, Vanessa. Forget it. I'll be there."

Before Mom is even at the car, she's got the cell phone out and pressed against her ear. She turns back and waves at me and Grandma.

We stand there long after Mom's car has left the driveway.

Grandma pushes the heavy door closed and picks up her Publix bag. When she grabs my hand, her skin feels soft and loose. "Come on, dear."

"Where are we going?" I don't have the energy to move and my wrist is killing me.

"You'll see."

I allow her to drag me into the kitchen while I hold my cast above my head. *Elevate, dear. Elevate.*

"Look." Grandma opens the bag to reveal two pints of Ben & Jerry's ice cream, a jar of rainbow-colored sprinkles, a squeeze bottle of fudge sauce, and a canister of whipped cream.

"Grandma," I say, "it's not even ten in the morning. I haven't had breakfast yet. Isn't it a little early for ice cream sundaes?"

Grandma looks at me and snorts. *That's where I get that from!* "Vanessa! First rule of life, dear: It's never too early for ice cream sundaes. Second rule of life: When confused about whether or not it's too early for ice cream sundaes, refer to rule number one. For goodness' sake, it's not like I pulled out a bottle of vodka."

I don't want to laugh, but I do.

Grandma hands me a bowl piled with everything, then creates her own ice cream masterpiece.

Mrs. Perez is off today or I'm sure she'd suggest I eat oatmeal instead.

Grandma and I clink spoons and dig in.

"What do you want to do this weekend?" Grandma asks, slurping up a dollop of whipped cream. "Movie? Museum? Concert? The world is your oyster, my dear." She looks at my cast and says, "Although I guess bowling is out of the question."

"Bowling is definitely out," I say, wiping my mouth. "But so is everything else, Grandma. I've got to study."

"Study? It's Saturday. Don't you think you deserve a little fun? Maybe invite that friend of yours over. What's her name?"

"Emma."

"Yes, would you like to call her and see if she can sleep over tonight? I'm sure your mother would approve of that."

"That would be fun, but—"

"We can watch movies and order pizza."

"I'd love to do that some other weekend, but—"

"And maybe we could polish each other's nails and fix each other's hair and—"

"Grandma, listen to me. The County Bee is Monday. *OHMYGOD! This Monday!* I need to study every spare minute. Besides, Emma has an equestrian event all day Saturday and is spending Sunday with her cousins who are visiting. So she couldn't sleep over."

"Oh. Then maybe you and I can . . ." Her voice trails off.

"You can help me study."

Grandma tilts her head and taps her finger to her chin. "Why not?"

We clink spoons again, and I realize my wrist is throbbing less. "Grandma, I think ice cream is good for my wrist."

"Of course it is," says Grandma. "All that calcium and everything. Let me get you some more."

17

I open my jewelry box and touch the bumblebee pin I got at last year's Regional Bee, the one after the County Bee. I lost that competition during round eight on the word "sagacious"—shrewd and wise. I certainly wasn't!

"This year," I proclaim, holding my bumblebee pin high, "I'm going all the way." *OHMYGOD! Did I just say that?*

I study words from my vocabulary notebooks until Grandma comes in. Then she quizzes me for hours. As I say each word, spell it, and say it again, I imagine myself on stage at the Scripps National Spelling Bee in Washington, D.C. I march up to the microphone and—here's the best part—I don't trip. In my imagination, I'm all grace and good spelling. Mom's in the front row, watching me spell the winning word, something long and difficult that 99.9 percent of the population never heard of. When I get it right and win the bee, Mom jumps from her seat and cheers.

I have to make it to the National Bee!

During our practice session, when I start to slur words, Grandma declares, "We need a break, Vanessa."

"Can't," I say, my right leg pumping. "It's only five o'clock. Give me another word."

"Only five o'clock? You've been at this all day, dear. Your mind seems a little addled."

"Addled. A-d-d-l-e-d. Addled."

"You're making me nervous, Vanessa."

"Nervous. N-e-r-v-o-u-s. Nervous." My leg moves up and down so fast that even when I lay my palm on it, it keeps bobbing like it's motorized. (Motorized. M-O-T-O-R-I-Z-E-D. Motorized.) "Next word, Grandma. Give me the next word."

"Restaurant," Grandma says firmly.

"Restau—"

"Come on." Grandma stands. "I'm taking you out to eat. Now. What's your favorite restaurant?"

It takes great restraint to keep from spelling "Hurricane Jeanne's." I say, "They have awesome salads and four kinds of soup every day."

"Hurricane Jeanne's it is," says Grandma. "Ice cream sundaes go only so far. I'm famished."

"Famished. F-a-m-i-s—"

"Stop!" Grandma holds her hands over her ears as if her head is about to explode.

I have that effect on people sometimes.

In the restaurant, I close my eyes and spell words from the menu. I eavesdrop on conversations and silently spell those words, too. And I keep one of my spelling notebooks on my lap during dinner and glance at it when Grandma isn't looking.

"Vanessa Rothrock?"

I turn and see a woman holding on to a squirming toddler. "Yes?"

"I hate to bother you"—the woman nods at Grandma—"but I read about you winning your school spelling bee in the newspaper."

She wants an autograph.

"And, well—" The little boy yanks on her arm. "One minute, Jacob. It's just that I competed in bees when I was your age. Got all the way to Regionals one year."

"That's wonderful," I say, squirreling bread in my cheek.

"Yes." She looks away for a moment, like she's seeing a memory. "I studied hundreds of words, thousands, but in round five, they gave me one word I never studied—'tintinnabular.' "

"Tintinnabular?" I repeat, dropping my fork.

"Tintinnabular," she says. "Of or relating to bells or the ringing of bells."

"I'm really sorry," I say to the woman. *How do you spell it? One "n" or two? OHMYGOD! I'm having a dictionary emergency here.*

"Don't be. That was a long time ago. I just hope you go all the way."

What is it with people and that phrase? I smile as the woman is dragged off by her toddler.

"Grandma, we have to go."

"Vanessa," she says, waving her spoon at me, "you haven't eaten your soup yet."

"Grandma, unless the cook has a dictionary in the back, we need to get home—or at least to a bookstore. I need to study!"

"I thought we'd been over that, dear. You studied all day. Now eat your soup." Grandma taps her spoon on the edge of her bowl. "And don't worry."

I think of the woman who still regrets losing the Regional Bee. I think of getting on the stage in front of hundreds of people on Monday. I think of the thousands of words I haven't studied yet, like "tintinnabular."

I'm worried.

18

Monday comes too quickly. Even though I barely slept all weekend and studied constantly, I feel utterly unprepared. There are so many words I didn't get to.

Grandma sits next to me in the car on the way to the County Bee. Her hand is on top of mine, which is on top of my leg. The leg that is pumping up and down faster than a piston. (Piston. P-I-S-T-O-N. Piston.)

Grandma takes a deep breath and presses my hand. "Worried, dear?"

My leg doesn't stop pumping. "Whatever gave you that idea?" I chew at the skin beside my thumbnail. "When's Mom coming?"

Grandma sighs. "I already told you. Your mother said she's having trouble getting a flight—"

"What kind of trouble?" I ask, my leg about to drill a hole through the floor of the car.

"I don't know." Grandma pats my hand. "She said she'll get here as soon as she can."

"Before the bee starts?"

"I don't know." Grandma smoothes her gray hair, which won't be tamed because it's kinky and wild like mine. "Would you like me to quiz you, Vanessa? Would that help you . . . relax?"

Relax! In the time it takes me to answer, I think that "quiz" is worth twenty-two points in Scrabble, forty-four if it's on a double word space and sixty-six if it's on a triple. "No," I say, "I don't think it will help me relax." *I don't think anything will help me relax.* "Thanks, though. I'm just a little nervous."

Grandma folds her hands in her lap and looks forward. "I couldn't tell."

My cell phone rings, and I fumble in my purse to find it. I hope it's Mom. "Hello?"

"Hi, Vanessa," Emma whispers. "Did I catch you before the bee?"

"Yes. Where are you?"

"Student services. I told Mrs. Durlofsky I had to call my mom because I forgot my lunch." Emma's voice gets even quieter. "But I really have money in my pocket." She chuckles softly. "Anyway, how are you? Nervous?"

I hunch toward the window to give myself a modicum of privacy. "Um, very."

"I'm sure. I'd be a wreck." Emma pauses, and I wonder if she wishes she were going to the County Bee instead of me. "But I know you'll do great."

"You think so?" I ask, biting the skin beside my thumb-nail.

"Of course you will. You're a spelling whiz."

Whiz. *Nineteen points in Scrabble.* "Thanks. By the way, how did your horse thingy go on Saturday?"

"My horse thingy? You mean my competition?"

We both giggle. Emma always makes me laugh when I need it most.

"I'll have you know," Emma says in a snooty tone, "I placed second overall for my age category."

"That's great, Em—"

"I'd better go. The secretary is giving me the evil eye. Good luck, Vanessa. I'll talk to you when you get back. After you win!"

"As if! Thanks, Emma."

Our car stops in front of a building and Grandma leaps out. "You're not supposed to—" I begin. But Grandma is already at the steps.

While I wait for Mr. Martinez, I pull a piece of paper from my purse. It's the fax Mom sent last night. It contains three words—four, if you stretch out the contraction. "I'll bee there." I kiss the paper and squeeze it to my heart.

After Mr. Martinez opens my door, I join Grandma and the three of us walk inside the building.

"Do you know where we go?" Grandma asks, gripping my right hand.

A girl points at us and whispers to her mother behind her hand. I turn away. I know she's not saying I'm a good speller. Or that I've got a cast on my wrist. She's saying I'm the daughter of the governor, of the *woman* running for president. My shoulders slump. *Can't I go anywhere and just be me, Vanessa big-feet, no-boobs, incurably clumsy Rothrock?*

"Vanessa!"

"Yes, Grandma. Sorry. I think we go in here."

It turns out Grandma has to leave me in a room with the other spellers. Mr. Martinez stands at the back of the room. I find a seat next to a girl who's talking quietly to herself.

"Hi," I say, hoping she's not put off by my having a security guard.

"Epidural," she says. "E-p-i-d-u-r-a-l. Epidural." Then she looks up. "Hi."

"What school are you—"

Without waiting for me to finish my sentence, the girl bends her head and talks to herself again. "Where was I? Epidural. E-p-i . . ."

A woman stands in front of the room and explains the rules. "There are a hundred of you now, and when this is over in a couple of hours, there will be only four remaining."

Four?

"Those children will go to the regional spelling bee, which will be held in exactly eight days."

Sweat erupts from my pits. *Four left. Eight days.* I can't breathe.

Onstage, behind the closed curtain, I'm seated near the back, fidgeting with the number card hanging from my neck. I notice it's the same number upside down—88. But I can't decide if this is a good omen or not. I panic about being seated so far back. I'll have farther to walk to the microphone, which means more opportunities to trip. Maybe it won't be so bad. Maybe I'll break my other wrist and then Mom will stay home for good. *Or will she?*

I hear pulleys and watch the curtains part. I crane my neck to see around the head of the person in front of me and squint.

We are announced. The audience applauds.

When my number is called, I make it to the front of the stage without tripping. There are a sea of people in the audience, way more than at the school bee. And they're all staring at me! Even though I don't move, my heart feels like it's going to fly from my chest. This must be how Mom feels when she's about to give a speech.

When I spot Grandma, I raise my cast slightly. I squint and notice strangers on either side of her. My shoulders sag.

"Number eighty-eight!"

I look around.

"Ahem. Number eighty-eight."

"Oh, that's me," I mumble into the microphone. "Sorry."

"Your word is 'atrophy.' "

Easy word, I think. The audience bubbles with laughter, and I realize I did more than think it. My face heats up. "Sorry," I say again. I want nothing more than to scamper back to my seat and hide behind the heads of the other spellers. "Atrophy," the pronouncer repeats.

"Atrophy," I say, my heart hammering. In my head, I

think *a trophy, a trophy, a trophy.* "A . . . t-r-o-p-h-y. Atro-phy." I linger a moment and hear no buzzer. I raise my fist in triumph and knock the microphone stand over. I bend to pick it up and horrible screeches come from the speakers. Some lady rushes over, takes the microphone stand from me, and pats my shoulder. I slink back to my seat and hunch low. I'm too embarrassed to look, but I'm sure that back-stage, Mr. Martinez is stifling laughter.

I should be thinking about what a fool I made of myself. Or of the word I might get next. I should definitely be listen-ing to the other spellers. But all I can think about is Mom. I look at my cast and feel sorry for myself. *Why isn't she here? She promised. And I've got the fax to prove it. Maybe she is here, but couldn't get a seat next to Grandma. Maybe she's late and she'll be here by my second word. Maybe . . .* A buzzer drills through my thoughts. Another speller down.

As each round progresses, I watch kids disappear from the stage. Soon, even though I'm near the back, there's no one directly in front of me. The judges ask the remaining dozen of us to move to the front row of chairs. I've got a good view of the audience and I still don't see Mom.

I spell "ennui" and "tempeh" and "bouillon" and almost don't realize it when the fifth speller messes up on the word "chiropractor" by substituting an *e* for the last *o*. When I hear the error and then the buzzer, I wince.

The auditorium is quiet and then erupts in applause. I think I hear Grandma give a loud whoop. The announcer says a few things as I absorb the fact that I'm one of four spellers left. Me. Vanessa big-feet, no-boobs, incurably clumsy, great-at-spelling Rothrock. I'm going to the Regionals. I pump my fist in the air, but feel it hit something.

"Ouch!"

I turn to see a woman rubbing her shoulder and glaring at me.

"Sorry." *At least I didn't hit you with my cast.*

Grandma is in front of me now, gripping my good hand. "You did it, Vanessa. You did it!" She hugs me so hard I can't breathe.

Watch my cast.

"I knew you could," she says. "I knew it!"

"You helped."

"Oh, pshaw!" Grandma waves her hand. "You did this all yourself. You should be very proud."

I am proud, but mostly I'm worried. I look beyond Grandma and see the other winners surrounded by their parents. "Where's Mom?"

The look on Grandma's face provides my answer. "Your mother called, dear, right before the bee. She couldn't—"

I don't hear the rest because I'm running. I'm off the stage and in the empty room where the girl was spelling "epidural" just a couple of hours ago. I rip my number off and hurl it. Then I run again, past people in the lobby, and push open the glass doors. Cool air feels good on my hot cheeks. I sit on the stone wall next to the stairs and catch a glimpse of Mr. Martinez only a few feet away. *I will not cry. I will not cry.* I cover my face. And cry. *How could she not come?*

Just as I'm pulling Mom's fax out of my purse to shred, I hear: "Vanessa?" I glance up, thinking it must be Mr. Martinez.

"Are you okay?"

I blink twice. Michael Dumas is standing in front of me. I almost don't recognize him because he's wearing a suit and tie. But then his eyelid starts twitching behind his glasses, and I know it's him.

I brush off my wet cheeks. "I'm fine." *How did you get here? Are you stalking me or something?* "What are you doing here?"

He points to the girl who was spelling "epidural." "My sister," he says. "She goes to Emerald Lakes Middle?"

I tilt my head. *You have a sister?*

"She wanted to go to public school." He leans in closer. "She thinks Lawndale Academy is elitist." Michael shrugs.

"Oh," I say, wishing Michael would go away. His eyelid is twitching like crazy.

"You sure you're okay, Vanessa?"

Why is Michael Dumas being so nice? This makes me want to cry more. A woman and a man, who must be Michael's mother and father, walk over. Mr. Martinez takes a step closer. *Great! Maybe the whole world can watch me cry. Let's get a few reporters in here, too.* I swipe at my eyes and wish everyone would go away and leave me alone.

"I'm fine," I say. "Really. I guess it was just too much. The bee and everything." I don't tell him that "everything" means worrying about Mom.

Michael's mother nods. She touches my knee and I jerk back, nearly falling off the stone wall.

"Oh!" Michael's father reaches for me, but I manage to right myself.

"I'm okay," I say. "Just nerves."

"Where is your, um . . ."

Grandma walks through the glass doors, spots me, and hurries over. "There you are, dear. I was looking all over for you."

"Grandma, this is Michael Dumas and his mother and father and epi—um, sister."

"Nice to meet you," Grandma says, reaching for their hands, one after the other.

Hey, maybe she should run for president. Then Mom could stay home with me.

"Vanessa," Grandma says, "we really must get back now."

Good.

Michael nudges his mother. She nods at him and says to Grandma, "We're taking the kids out to celebrate Marigold's making it to the County Bee."

Marigold? Michael's sister's name is Marigold? Did they want another "M" name and thought "Megan" and "Madison" were too plain? Maybe Michael's mother was under a heavy dose of epidural when she named her. At least my mom didn't name me after a flower, a bush, or a tree. I feel a tear slip out. Mom. Didn't you know how much this meant to me?

Michael's mother continues: "And we'd love it if you'd join us."

I hold my breath. The last thing on earth I'd like to do is go out for ice cream with Michael Dumas and his twitching eyelid, not to mention his parents and his sister, the flower.

"Well . . . ," Grandma says, stealing a glance at me. I know she's thinking about sinking her dentures into a nice cold bowl of ice cream.

No, Grandma! I think as hard as I can. *Don't do it! Just say no!*

Grandma must read my mind, because she says, "I'm sorry. We really must get back."

Michael's mouth turns down and his shoulders slump.

"We understand," says his father in this cool French accent. I wonder why Michael doesn't have a French accent.

"Maybe another time," says his mother. "And Vanessa?"

"Yes?"

"Congratulations on making it to the Regional Bee. That's quite an accomplishment."

I stop myself from spelling "accomplishment." "Thank you." Then I look at Michael and shrug. "Sorry, Michael. Maybe some other time."

He nods and turns away.

Grandma scoots next to me in the back of the car, and Mr. Martinez drives away.

"Miss your mother?" Grandma asks, patting my knee.

"No," I say. *Liar.*

"Well, I'm sure she feels terrible about not being able to be here."

"Whatever."

"Vanessa?"

"It's just that I seem to come last on her list of priorities."

"Honey, your mother is running for president. There are a slew of primaries tomorrow. Do you know what that means?"

I turn my head and look out the window. *I know exactly what that means.* "That she can't ever come to watch me in spelling bees anymore."

"Vanessa!"

"Well, she can't. She probably won't even be there when I get to the Nationals."

Grandma touches my shoulder, but I pull away.

"Vanessa, what your mother is doing is important to her. To the country. To the world." Grandma takes my chin in her hand so I have to look at her. "We all have to make sacrifices so she can do this."

"Why do I have to make sacrifices?" I ask. "I'm not running for president. I didn't ask for"—I nod toward Mr. Martinez in the front seat—"any of this."

Grandma takes a deep breath. "Vanessa, there are some things greater than ourselves, some things worth sacrificing for."

"Yeah," I mutter, "but I'm the only one who seems to be sacrificing around here." I lay my cast on the armrest and look out the window.

Grandma heaves a big sigh, but I don't look at her.

We ride back to the mansion in silence.

I'm on the edge of my bed, my back to Mom. I'd fold my arms across my chest, but my cast gets in the way.

Mom comes around and kneels in front of me. "Nessa?"

I whip my head in the other direction.

"Please look at me."

Why should I?

"Vanessa!"

I pretend to look at Mom, but really I stare at the place just above her eyebrows. Her forehead is wrinkled.

"Vanessa." Her breath smells like coffee and breath mints. "The mayor wanted to meet with me. There was no other time. I had to push my flight back—"

"And miss my bee! You promised you'd be there." I pull out the rumpled fax with her words: "I'll bee there."

She puts her hand on my knee.

I turn away. "Are you going to treat your campaign

promises the same way? Only fulfill them when it's convenient?"

Mom stands. "I can't talk to you when you're like this."

I press my lips together. *Then don't talk to me.*

Mom smoothes her skirt and says quietly, "I have a very important meeting this afternoon. If you want to talk, I'll be available at dinner."

Available at dinner? Who does she think she is? President of the United States? I gulp. *Almost.*

When Mom leaves, I pace. It does nothing to dissipate (Dissipate. D-I-S-S-I-P-A-T-E. Dissipate.) my anger. *Is it so wrong to want Mom to myself? At least some of the time?* I open one of my spelling notebooks, but can't focus. I pace more. *Why can't she wait until I'm in college to do this? I deserve at least one parent at home, don't I?* I think of Dad, then shake my head.

I grab a pile of letters from my desk. There seems to be more fan mail than ever. I decide to read through the letters, since there's nothing else to do. Besides, reading those letters always cheers me up.

Dear Vanessa Rothrock,

    I wish my mom were more like yours. I see her on TV all the time talking about education and reading with kids and stuff. My mom says I'd better learn to work with my hands and stop worrying about books.

    But I love to read. I spend every lunch period at the school library.

Do you love to read? If you do, what do you love to read?
Sincerely,
Robert Martin

I sigh and pick up my purple pen.

Dear Robert,
    Thank you for your letter. I think it's wonderful that you love to read. Books can take you many places.
    I love reading, too. When I'm studying for spelling bees, I read mostly dictionaries and word lists. But when the bees are over, I enjoy reading historical fiction and biographies.
    Robert, every year on my birthday, my mom takes me to the bookstore and allows me to buy any book I want. I think you should get to do this, too.
    Happy reading,
    Vanessa Rothrock

I reach into the purple pouch in my jewelry box and pull out a twenty-dollar bill. I paper-clip the money to the letter and write a note to go with it:

Mr. Adams,
Please include a gift certificate to a bookstore near this boy's home. The money is from my allowance.
Thank you,
Vanessa

I already feel a little better by the time I pull out the next letter in my pile.

There is a yellow sticky note on the outside of the envelope: "S.S." I try to figure out what "S.S." stands for as I reach into the open envelope. *Silly Stuff* or *Sophisticated Selection* or *Spectacularly Stupid*. I snort as I pull out the letter.

> **Governor Rothrock,**
>
> **Don't think you'll get away with trying to keep guns from people who want them. I've got the NRA behind me. And all you've got is your liberal, lefty views.**
>
> **I don't care if you're a woman. I'll put you in your place if you try to mess with gun owners. I have a right to bear arms. It says so in the constitutional declarational.**
>
> **You won't ever get my gun, but my gun might get you!**
>
> **Signed,**
>
> **NOT your biggest fan!**

"Ohmygod!"

I realize the letter could be laced with anthrax or something and fling it to the floor. It looks menacing against the purple carpet. I thump my forehead, suddenly understanding what the "S.S." stands for. This letter was supposed to go to the Secret Service. It must have gotten mixed into my pile of letters by mistake. *Does Mom know about this? I've got to show it to her, tell her she's in danger.*

I find my tweezers and pick the letter up with them. My

hand shakes, making it hard to hang on to the letter, but I do. I rush down the stairs holding the letter out in front. I trip on the last step, breaking my fall with my right hand. It hurts, but I don't care. I pick up the letter again—*Mom!*—and rush toward her office.

Ms. Purdy, Mom's assistant, sits at her big oak desk as usual. Mom and I call her the Gatekeeper because it's her job to keep people out of Mom's office unless they have an appointment.

"Ms. Purdy," I gasp. "I have . . . to see . . . my mom. It's . . . an emergency."

Ms. Purdy eyes the letter I'm holding way in front of me. I whip it behind my back.

"I'm sure it is, Vanessa. But your mother is in an important meeting until"—she looks at the clock on her desk—"five. She asked not to be disturbed."

I have to show Mom the letter. She's in danger. What could she be meeting about that's so important? What color to paint the State Dining Room?

"As soon as she comes out of the meeting, I'll tell her you need to talk to her."

"Thanks, Ms. Purdy." I feel my shoulders sink. *Thanks, Ms. Purdy? Mom's life is in danger here. She'd rescue me. Wouldn't she?* "Uh, Ms. Purdy?"

"Yes?"

I don't answer. I bolt toward Mom's office door. Unfortunately, I have to turn the brass handle with the hand that's casted, since I'm holding the tweezers in my right hand. I manage to open the door just as Ms. Purdy's pudgy fingers plunge into my shoulder.

"Mom!"

Mom looks up from behind her huge desk. Her eyes widen.

The man in the big leather chair facing Mom turns to see what's going on. I drop my tweezers.

"I'm so sorry, Governors," Ms. Purdy says. "I tried to tell her—"

Mom holds up a hand. "Thank you, Ms. Purdy. Vanessa, come here, please."

I pick up the letter with my tweezers and walk toward Mom's desk. As I pass her guest I curtsy—*OHMYGOD!*—and say, "Hello, Governor Schwarzenegger. I'm so sorry—"

Governor Arnold Schwarzenegger stands. I look up and realize that this man has the squarest head I've ever seen. *It's a perfect rhomboid.* He offers me his massive hand. I drop the letter and tweezers on Mom's desk and offer him my right hand, afraid he's going to crush all twenty-seven bones in it. But he barely squeezes and says, "No problem." He turns to Mom. "I assume this is your lovely daughter."

Mom sighs. "It is. Governor Schwarzenegger, this is Vanessa. Vanessa"—she sweeps her arm—"Governor Schwarzenegger."

I curtsy again. *Strike me dead before I embarrass myself further.*

"Please don't worry," he says, his Austrian accent thick. "I've got four of my own at home."

Yeah, and Maria Shriver is home taking care of them. I shake the thought from my mind. "Mom. Governor Schwarzenegger . . ." I curtsy again. *Somebody shoot me. The letter!* "It's an emergency or I wouldn't have barged in. You have to read this letter. Now."

"Vanessa, we're—"

"It's a matter of life and death."

Mom picks up the letter and I want to tell her to use the tweezers—just in case—but I don't. Suddenly her mouth opens.

I knew it. I knew it was really scary. Now she'll pull out of the campaign. Maybe she'll even stop being governor.

"How did you . . . where did you . . . get this?"

"It was mixed in with my mail."

Mom slams her palm on the desk. "That's unacceptable. I'm going to talk with Mr. Adams. You should never have seen this. They need to be more careful."

But I did see it.

Then that deep voice I remember loving in *Twins* says, "What is it, Elyssa? May I?"

Governor Schwarzenegger reads the letter. Then the most surprising sound comes from him. Laughter. "Oh, this one isn't so bad," he says, covering his mouth. "You should have seen the ones I got during the budget crunch. I think half the state wanted to pummel me to death with oranges."

When Mom laughs, too, I'm shocked. *This isn't funny!*

"Ever since I declared my intention to run," Mom says, "I've received dozens a day. And the number really escalated after I won the Iowa caucuses and the New Hampshire primary."

"I know what you mean," says Governor Schwarzenegger. "I really get a kick out of the ones done in crayon. I have to tell you, a threat letter written in periwinkle is not very intimidating."

Mom bites her lower lip. "No, I guess it's not."

Have I missed some important element of the conversation? How did a threatening letter become hilarious? "What's so funny?" I barely peep. Of course, no one hears me, so I have to belt it out. "What's so funny?"

"Oh, Nessa. These letters come in daily. They're all forwarded to the Secret Service. Believe me, sweetheart, they pursue all credible threats."

"Credible threats?"

"You know," Mom says, "letters from people who might really carry out what's in their letters."

I gasp.

"Don't worry, Nessa. That almost never happens. And I've got round-the-clock protection."

I'm worried.

"And so do you," she finishes. I know Mom is talking about Mr. Martinez and the other guards who are in the mansion every day. Mom nods toward Governor Schwarzenegger. "Now, since the governor flew all the way from California, do you mind if we finish our meeting?"

"Meeting?" I still don't get why this letter isn't a bigger deal. The writer practically said he's planning to shoot Mom.

Mom gives me a look and checks her watch. "We'll talk more about this at dinner."

"One more thing," Governor Schwarzenegger says, and I'm absolutely sure he's going to tell me some horrid story about a governor who received threatening letters and was then assassinated. "Come here, Vanessa."

My heart thumps.

The governor grabs a pen from Mom's desk and holds it over my cast. "May I?"

Arnold Schwarzenegger wants to sign my cast! There are some perks to being the governor's daughter. "Yes!"

He writes, "To Vanessa, a courageous girl. Arnold Schwarzenegger."

OHMYGOD! I will have to casually lay my cast across Reginald's desk in school. He'll think this is so cool. And Emma will absolutely flip.

Someone clears her throat. It's Mom. I realize I've been staring at my cast entirely too long.

"Thanks," I say.

"Vanessa?" Mom says it more like a command than a question.

I know she means it, so I back out of her office, curtsying all the way. Then I blurt with a thick accent: "I'll be back!"

"Vanessa!"

"No I won't." I duck out and shut the heavy door. I can

hear you-know-who laughing on the other side. *I made Arnold Schwarzenegger laugh and I didn't even trip.*

"Vanessa?"

Ms. Purdy drums pudgy fingers on her desk.

"Sorry about that, Ms. Purdy." I half-bow, half-curtsy as I back out of her office. "Sorry." I touch the place where Governor Schwarzenegger signed my cast, then run all the way back up to the Purple Palace.

Once my heart stops pounding, I wonder why Mom and Governor Schwarzenegger weren't panicked about that letter.

I am.

20

On Tuesday at lunch, Emma touches the place where Arnold Schwarzenegger signed my cast. "Vanessa," she says, "you are so lucky. I wish I'd broken my arm. I mean . . ."

We both laugh.

She draws a perfect ladybug near the edge of my cast and signs, "Friends forever, Emma."

I wish I could draw like Emma.

"Congrats, too, on winning the County Bee. I knew you would."

I duck my head. "Thanks. It was pretty cool." I don't tell Emma how sad I was that Mom wasn't there.

"What's wrong?"

"Huh?" *Can Emma read my thoughts?*

"You've only taken one bite of your sandwich and I'm nearly finished with mine."

Should I tell her what's bothering me? "Emma, do you know what today is?"

She swallows. "Tuesday. Right?"

"Duh," I say, nudging her shoulder. "But it's also the day that primaries will be held in eight different states."

"Oh, of course," Emma says as though she watches the news all day long. Then she tilts her head. "So?"

"So, if my mom wins most of them, she might have a really good chance to run for president."

"And that's fantastic, right? Do you think she'll do well?"

I let out a big breath. "Emma, I know this is really important to my mom and all, but . . ." I lower my head. "I kind of don't want her to win her party's nomination."

"*What?*" Emma says entirely too loudly. "Why not?"

I look around to make sure no one is staring and I whisper, "I don't know. She'll be too busy"—I feel tears prick the corners of my eyes—"for me."

"Oh, Vanessa." Emma puts her arm around my shoulders. "She'll be here for you. Your mom is way cool. Remember that fifties party she threw for your birthday when you turned ten? And the time she took us on a weekend cruise because we both ended the school year with all As? Besides, whatever happens, I'm always here for you." Emma gives my shoulders a squeeze.

I sniff. "I know."

"Anyway," she says, "think of all the cool benefits if your mom actually wins the nomination and then gets elected.

You could have a sleepover party . . . at the White House. Not to mention staff to fulfill your every whim. Ice cream sundaes at midnight. A private screening of your favorite movie. Maybe with the actual movie star sitting right next to you. Great, right?"

"Yeah, I guess." I hadn't really thought about the good things that could happen if Mom won.

"And you already get some pretty cool benefits just by being the governor's daughter." She taps my cast. "Like Arnold Schwarzenegger signing your cast."

"Yeah, I guess." I finish my sandwich and give Emma a hug before I go to my next class. But deep in the pit of my stomach, I'm still worried about the possibility of Mom doing really well in today's primaries.

After finishing my homework, studying vocabulary, and eating salad, baked salmon, and broccoli for dinner, I stay up late watching CNN. I bite the skin beside my thumbnail as the primary results come in. I raise my fist in triumph when Mom loses North Dakota. Unfortunately, that's followed by a win in Delaware. Soon the results from all eight states are in.

Grandma calls. "Isn't it wonderful, dear?"

I pretend to be excited. "It's great."

"Vanessa, I'm so proud of your mother right now, I feel like I'm going to burst."

"Don't do that, Grandma. You'll make a mess all over your condo."

"Aren't you funny? Vanessa, dear—"

I hear a beep and ask Grandma to hold on. It's Mom on the other line, so I hang up with Grandma.

"Vanessa, are you watching the results?" Mom's voice sounds hoarse, as though she's been screaming and straining her vocal cords all day.

"Yes," I say, my heart sinking.

"Isn't it wonderful?"

For you.

"I won five out of eight states. Couldn't have hoped for anything better. The momentum's really going now. Arnie says my numbers are through the roof."

"That's great, Mom. When are you coming home?"

Mom is quiet. "Vanessa, the schedule's going to be pretty grueling. Super Tuesday is in less than thirty days. And you know that will pretty much determine whether I secure enough primaries to win the nomination."

"I know."

"So, like we talked about, I'll be home for the big things, but not for tucking you in at night or most of your school events."

Or the County Bee. "I understand." *I just don't like it.*

"All right, sweetheart. I just wanted to share the great news with you. I've got to run."

I close my eyes. "Congrats, Mom."

"Thanks, Vanessa. That means a lot. I love you."

"Love you, too."

Wednesday morning, by the time I reach advisory, I've been congratulated by at least a dozen kids. I didn't think the kids at my school paid attention to the news at all, much less to politics. Emma gives me a hug in the hall and asks if I'm okay. I nod, thinking about how lucky I am to have a friend like Emma to get me through this.

In advisory, I draw a rhomboid around Governor Schwarzenegger's words because my cast is filling up with signatures from students and teachers. Even Mrs. Foster signed it. I decide not to let Coach Conner near it, but that's easy to do because I'm exempt (Exempt. E-X-E-M-P-T. Exempt.) from P.E. until the cast comes off.

When I show Reginald what Governor Schwarzenegger wrote, he says that's great, but he got Shaquille O'Neal's signature on his basketball sneakers.

Whoever that is!

Friday morning, there's an envelope in my locker with the familiar heart over the "a." My own heart rate quickens. I don't wait to open it, but turn my back to Mr. Martinez.

Vanessa,

> **Good luck at the Regional Bee.**
> **I know you'll do great.**

I wonder if Mr. Martinez could run a fingerprint check for me. But I'm pretty sure I know who's been dropping these notes in my locker.

I'm feeling so good from the extra attention I've been

getting all week that when I walk past Reginald's desk in advisory, I take a chance. "Thanks," I say, holding up the envelope.

Reginald looks at the envelope. "Thanks for what?"

"For the good wishes at the Regional Bee."

"Oh." He looks away from me. "I didn't give you that."

My brain scrambles. Is Reginald pretending not to have written the notes? Or—gasp!—maybe he isn't the one who's been dropping them into my locker. I rush to my seat, take out a textbook, and hide my face behind it. *OHMYGOD! How could I be so stupid? But if Reginald isn't dropping those notes into my locker, who is?*

21

I bob from foot to foot, spelling words in my head, like "terrified," "panicked," and "nauseated." By the time I walk onstage with the other spellers at the Regional Bee, I'm shaking. *Still yourself, Vanessa,* I hear in my mind. *Still yourself.*

"I can't," I whisper.

The boy next to me, Number 45, inches away.

I take a deep breath and look at the audience. Sitting next to Grandma in the front row is Mom. I elbow Number 45. "My mom's here. Right there." I hold up my purple cast covered with signatures and wiggle my fingers.

"That's nice," the boy says, rubbing the place on his arm where I elbowed him.

"Sorry," I mumble, then go back to paying attention to Mom. She's sitting tall like she's . . . proud. Of me! *We'll both make it to Washington, D.C. I'll make it to the National*

Bee and you'll make it to the White House. The White House? What am I thinking!

When they call my number, 44, I keep my eyes focused on Mom as I walk to the front of the stage. Somehow, Mom's grace travels through the air and seeps through my body, because I do not trip, stumble, or knock anything over.

My word is "aggrandize." I pronounce the word, spell it, and pronounce it again. No buzzer. Polite applause.

After two hours of spelling and sweating, sweating and spelling, I'm one of eight spellers left. I chew right through the skin beside my thumbnail. When they call the boy before me, my heart hammers.

The pronouncer says, "Your word is 'impetigo.' "

I snort. I don't realize how loud the snort was until the other spellers and the judges glare at me. I can't help it. I'm picturing me and Mom with impetigo—my idea for getting her to drop out of the race. I imagine the lesions on each of our faces. "Lucky," I say into my palm. "Wish I'd gotten that word."

After the boy asks for the meaning and the origin, and for the word to be used in a sentence, I get a feeling he's not as familiar with the word as I am. You can study a thousand, two thousand, ten thousand words, but if they give you one word you're not familiar with, it's all over. Just like what happened to that mother I met in the restaurant when I was out with Grandma. It takes only one unfamiliar word to obliterate (Obliterate. O-B-L-I-T-E-R-A-T-E. Obliterate.) months of study.

The boy sways from side to side and slowly says: "I-m-p-e-t-a-g-o." I wince when he makes the mistake and again when the buzzer sounds. The boy is dazed. Someone leads him offstage. I hear him crying.

When my number is called, I walk to the front of the stage, focus on Mom, and steel myself for my word.

The pronouncer says my word. My mind races. I squeeze my eyes shut and try to picture the word on a page in one of my dictionaries or in one of my spelling notebooks. If I had this word in one of my notebooks, it would be in the one marked "Unusual Words," but I'm positive the word is not in any of my notebooks.

I open my eyes and scan the audience. They're staring at me. I focus on Mom again. She's biting her thumbnail. Grandma's fist is pressed to her mouth. I hear someone in the audience whisper, "She doesn't know it."

I pull my shoulders back. *There's still a chance.* "May I have the definition, please?"

"A cookie that has been flavored with ginger and spice, then dusted with powdered sugar."

I think of Mrs. Perez and her lemon squares. (L-E-M-O-N S-Q-U-A-R-E-S.) Why couldn't she have made these cookies instead?

Take your time. Stall. "May I have the origin of the word, please?"

"German."

My stomach plunges. "Part of speech?"

"Noun."

I concentrate so hard my head feels like it's going to split. All I succeed in producing, though, is sweat, and it's pouring from my pits and from above my upper lip. I look at Mom, pleading.

She leans forward. Her eyes snap shut, and I know she's willing the correct spelling into my mind.

I close my eyes, ready to receive Mom's mental message. But there's too much interference. People are murmuring. Sweat drips down my body, and I feel the national bee slipping away.

The pronouncer clears his throat. *A bad sign.*

I clear my throat and say, "Pfeffernusse. F-e-f-f-e-r-n-u-s-s. Pfeffernusse."

When the buzzer sounds, I don't hear it. I assume that by some miracle of God I spelled the word correctly, and I head back toward my seat. Another speller gasps. The buzzer sounds again. This time, I hear it but can't make sense of it. I whirl around and look at the judges' table. The judges sit immobile, silent. I turn farther around and see Mom. Her hand is over her mouth. Then I understand. I slap my own hand to my own mouth and run offstage.

My head's between my knees and I'm hyperventilating when Mom and Grandma rush in. I consider telling Mom to dial 911 because I can't catch my breath and I'm pretty sure I'm going to die. At least I hope I will. How could I have blown the Regional Bee on a cookie?

I look around the room. Kids are bent over with parents

consoling them, too. "I worked so hard." *How did I end up in the losers' room?*

"It's okay, Vanessa," Mom says, her arms around me.

I nod, but can't speak. Because I know it definitely is not okay. I glance up and see Mom's entourage. (Entourage. E-N-T— Oh, for goodness' sake!) I don't feel like being surrounded by a gaggle of people right now. It's embarrassing enough just to be me. If Mom's press secretary dares to tell me what a good job I did, I'll scream!

Grandma squeezes my hand. "You did fantastic, sweetie. Absolutely fantastic."

Breathe, Vanessa. Breathe.

"You did, Vanessa." Mom's arms tighten around me. "You should be very proud of yourself. Very—"

Suddenly there's a crush of reporters in the room. Mom stands in front of me and puts her hands up, but before she can say anything, one of the reporters blurts, "Vanessa, sorry you lost. Looks like only your mom has a chance of going to Washington now."

Mom nods at Mr. Adams. That's all. Just a nod.

Mr. Adams escorts the reporter outside, and I know Mom will never call on *him* again at a press conference. Mr. Adams's assistant clears the room of the rest of the reporters and their camera crews, promising a comment later.

Mom stands and straightens her skirt. "You ready to go, baby?"

My heart does a little flip when Mom says that, because

"baby" is what Daddy used to call me. Mom's eyes are wet, but she's got on a brave smile. I look at my cast where Governor Schwarzenegger wrote that I'm courageous. I'm not courageous. Mom is. I'm afraid of everything.

"Mom?"

She looks me in the eyes. "Yes, Nessa?"

"Now that the bee is over, I'll have lots of extra time."

"You certainly will," Mom says, brushing a tear off my cheek. "Won't that be nice?"

"I'd like to help with your campaign."

Mom reels back as if pushed. "Nessa? That's a big change of heart."

Daddy always supported your campaigns. He would have wanted this for you. But since he's not here . . .

"Are you sure this is what you want?" Mom asks.

I nod.

"Because it could get time-consuming, and you might be exposed to some negative things."

I think of Mom and Dad prepping me for the bad publicity Mom might receive when she ran for reelection as governor by acting out different scenarios at the dinner table. "I know what to expect."

"I'm not sure you do." Mom ruffles my hair. "A presidential campaign is different from a gubernatorial one." She kneels in front of me and squeezes my good hand. "But I appreciate this more than you know." She stands and kisses my forehead. "I'll talk to Mr. Adams about it. I'm sure he can find ways for you to help."

We walk out together, Mom with her shoulders back and Grandma with her head held high: Team Rothrock. We walk right past those nosy reporters and get into the car.

And even though I just lost the Regional Spelling Bee because of a cookie, I feel surprisingly good.

22

After a radio interview during which I trip, fall on my cast, and scream on the air, Mr. Adams decides print media might be the best means for me to help with Mom's campaign.

I answer interview questions for teen magazines. When I complete a questionnaire, I return it to Mr. Adams for his staff to review before mailing it back to the magazine. I also answer lots of fan mail, some from adults. And I help stuff envelopes for mailings when I'm not too busy with school-work.

I take a short break from working on Mom's campaign to obsess with Emma about Valentine's Day.

"What chance is there," Emma asks at lunch, "that Reginald will give either of us a Valentine's Day card tomorrow?"

I wipe my mouth. "Um, zero?"

"No, seriously," Emma says.

"I am serious." I take another bite of my egg salad sandwich. "He likes Holly Stevens now. It's all over school."

"Yeah, I heard, but I also heard that she thinks he's totally immature."

We giggle.

"But where does that leave us?" Emma asks.

I take a swig of chocolate milk and think about it. "Remember when we were little and had to give every kid in class a Valentine's Day card?"

"Yeah," Emma says, twirling her hair around her finger. "Why don't we do that anymore? I liked those little cards. Remember the extra one in the package for the teacher?"

"Yeah. They were cool, and no one ever felt left out then."

Emma sips from her water bottle. "Those were the days."

"I know. Now it's all complicated."

Emma pushes me. "I have an idea."

"What?"

"Let's you and me give each other cards tomorrow. That way, if no one else gives us any, we still have the ones from each other." She tilts her head. "Deal?"

I extend my right hand, and we shake on it. "Deal."

When the bell rings, I stuff the rest of my sandwich, my empty milk carton, and my napkin into a bag and walk to the trash can. I notice Reginald leaving his trash on the table and walking away with his friends. On his way out of the cafeteria, he shoves Michael Dumas.

I shake my head and dump my garbage.

As I walk Emma to her class, I say, "I'm not even sure I want a Valentine's Day card from Reginald."

She looks at me like I'm crazy. "Yes you do."

"Okay, I do. But really, I'm not sure."

"Whatever." Emma ducks into class, and I rush off to language arts class. We're finishing reading *Romeo and Juliet* out loud today. Guess who is reading the part of Romeo? Reginald. And guess who is *not* reading the part of Juliet? Me, thank goodness. I read the part of the nurse. Carilynn. Winser, who is supposed to read Juliet's lines, is absent today so Mrs. Durlofsky reads her part. Every time Reginald has to say Romeo's lines to Mrs. Durlofsky, he squirms in his seat and mumbles. It's great. Everyone laughs, especially during the death scene.

At home after school, I realize Emma didn't say whether we should buy Valentine's Day cards for each other or make them, so I get out colored paper, a pair of scissors, a glue stick, and purple markers in three different shades. Cutting and gluing make me feel like a little kid again. Even though it's challenging because of the cast on my left arm, I have a good time.

I put on some music and work until dinnertime. When I'm finished, I've made cards for Mom, Grandma, and Mrs. Perez, and a big one for Emma. I sign Emma's card "BFF, Vanessa," put it in a big envelope, and draw purple hearts all over the outside.

There is definitely excitement in the air at school because it's Valentine's Day. The girls giggle with their friends at their lockers and the guys stand around, trying to act cool. I bet the boys secretly hope to get Valentine's Day cards, too.

I stop at my locker to drop off some books, then meet Emma at her locker before advisory just as we'd planned.

I pull the card I made Emma from my backpack and give it to her.

"Oh," she says after she opens the envelope, "you made it. I should have made the one for you." She reads the card and hugs me. "Thanks. I love it. Now here's the one I got you." She hands me a medium-sized pink envelope.

The card has a teddy bear on the front, and it reminds me of the birthday card Daddy gave me on my eighth birthday. I get a pang in my stomach and quickly read Emma's card out loud to keep from thinking about Daddy. "I'm bear-y glad we're friends." I open it and read the words on the inside. "Happy Valentine's Day. Here's a big bear hug for you."

"Thanks." I give Emma a squeeze.

Emma looks up at Mr. Martinez, then takes a step away and leans into my ear. "Guess which boy gave me a Valentine's Day card today?"

My heart beats fast and I look around at the kids in the hall, wondering which boy gave Emma a card. "Who?" I practically shout.

She lets out a big breath. "My little brother."

"Oh." My shoulders sag.

"And I know my mom really bought the card *and* signed his name. Real exciting Valentine's Day, huh?"

"Sorry," I say. "But you still might get a card from someone today. You never know." I poke her in the arm.

"Yeah, maybe. Did you get any cards beside mine so far today?"

I tell Emma about the Valentine's Day card Grandma sent me with twenty dollars inside. I tell Emma about the gigantic card from Mom that was at my place at the kitchen table this morning along with a set of purple pens, pencils, and erasers. I do *not* tell Emma about the card that was inside my locker this morning, the one I quickly read and shoved into my backpack.

The handwriting inside that card said:

Dear Vanessa,
   I hope you have a fantastic Valentine's Day. You deserve it.
   Signed,
   Your Secret Admirer

Just thinking of the card gives me goose bumps and I really want to tell Emma about it. Together, we might be able to figure out who my secret admirer is, but I don't want to make her feel bad.

"See you at lunch," Emma says.

"Yeah," I say. "Maybe by then you'll have gotten a card." *And then I can share the one I got with you.*

"Yeah, maybe."

I don't get any more cards the rest of the day. And no one comes up and tells me he is my secret admirer. I hope it's not a mean joke.

By the time I get home, there is a huge pile of fan letters I need to reply to, along with a questionnaire from a magazine. I get so busy, I don't have time to think about Valentine's Day anymore, or my secret admirer, or even whether I remembered to eat dinner or not. (I didn't, unless a lemon square and a glass of milk count as dinner.)

I stay extremely busy helping with Mom's campaign until early March, when ten states hold their primaries on the same day. That's why I feel like I made a huge difference in Mom's winning six of the ten states on Super Tuesday. Six out of ten is really good, Mom tells me. Yay, us!

The morning after Super Tuesday, I do twice as many exercises as usual in the shower and say a really long prayer to the Boob Fairy. If Mom wins her party's nomination and becomes president, I want to make sure I'm wearing at least a B cup to the inauguration.

Mom takes a short break from campaigning to spend time on Florida business and on being with me.

"Hey, Mom," I say, like we have breakfast together every morning.

She looks up from her coffee and newspapers, a big grin on her face. "Hey yourself."

"Mom, you're absolutely glowing from winning so many primaries."

"Still more work to do," she says, taking her mug to the sink. " 'Miles to go before I sleep.' But I think I'm pretty safe now in considering a running mate."

"A running mate? You? Mom! You think it's too much exercise when you get a run in your pantyhose."

Mom laughs so hard she actually spits on me. *Why do I have to be so funny?*

"Nessa, I'm talking about choosing a vice presidential candidate to run on the ticket with me."

My cheeks heat up. "I knew that." *I so didn't know that.*

Mom gives me a kiss on the forehead and checks her watch. "You'd better grab something to eat and get to school." She pats me on the behind, turns back to her newspaper, and mutters, "Run in my pantyhose. Good one."

On the ride to school, I think about how happy Mom looked. *She hasn't looked this happy since before Daddy died. Campaigning agrees with her.*

At my locker, I'm still beaming from Mom's good mood when I see Michael Dumas coming toward me.

"Hi, Vanessa," he says.

"Hi," I say, raising my left arm, surprised at how light it feels without the cast. The skin where the cast was is pale and blotchy, so I put my arm down right away.

"You got your cast off."

"Yes." I wait for Michael to leave, but he doesn't. "It

was kind of scary when the orthopedist pulled out his little round saw. But just like he told me, it didn't hurt. Just vibrated."

"That's good. 'Good Vibrations.' Get it?"

I most certainly do not.

Michael clears his throat. "Anyway, I'm glad it didn't hurt, Vanessa. You going to be excused from doing stuff in P.E. the rest of the year?"

I wish! Michael's eyelid begins to quiver, and I want to leave before it escalates into a full-blown twitch, but instead I look more closely at his eyes. *Something is different.* "Michael?"

He pulls his shoulders back. "Contacts. You like?"

"They're . . ." I knew Michael had nice green eyes, but without his glasses in the way, I can see they are absolutely . . . gorgeous. "They're—they're nice," I stammer.

"Mom and Dad got contacts for me as a birthday gift."

"You look good without glasses." *OHMYGOD! Did I just tell Michael Dumas he looks good without glasses?*

"Thanks, Vanessa."

I nod like I've seen the cool kids do.

"Hey, Vanessa, would you like to—"

"Ms. Rothrock." Mr. Martinez is next to me, tapping his watch. "You really should be getting to class."

Sometimes I forget there's a security guard standing within inches, ready to embarrass me at a moment's notice. I nod at Mr. Martinez, whisper "Sorry" to Michael, and turn my attention to the combination on my locker.

Michael walks off.

What was he going to ask me?

Inside my locker, an envelope rests on top of my textbooks. I grab it along with two textbooks and rush to advisory—trailed, of course, by the sound of Mr. Martinez's shoes tap-tapping on the linoleum behind me.

While Mr. Applebaum sits behind his desk at the front of the room, I examine the envelope. There's no heart over the "a" in my name. In fact, there's no name at all. *Was this meant for me?*

I open the envelope, read the letter, and think: *This can't be meant for me. That's why there was no name on the envelope.* But then I read the words again and I know it is.

I raise my hand. Mr. Applebaum doesn't look up from his desk. I clear my throat and wave my hand. He still doesn't look up. I drop my math textbook flat on the floor. He looks at me. So does the rest of the class.

I'm not sure how I manage to speak, but I do. "May I please be excused?"

Mr. Applebaum nods at the hall pass hanging by the door, grunts, and goes back to whatever he's working on.

With the envelope clutched in my hand, I rush from the classroom. *Slow, Vanessa. Calm down.* I turn to Mr. Martinez as I'm walking. "Bathroom," I say in explanation. He nods and continues to follow. *Should I give him the envelope? Of course I should, but I can't!*

In the bathroom stall, I pull the letter from the envelope again. I can't catch my breath. Mom and Governor

Schwarzenegger were wrong. Threatening letters aren't remotely funny.

I take a deep breath and read the letter again.

Vanessa,

If you think losing the regional spelling bee was bad, wait till you see what I'm going to do if your mommy doesn't drop out of the race. You're a smart girl. I'm sure you'll think of something to convince her to drop out. Because if you don't . . .

I'm keeping an eye on things. A close eye! So don't even think about telling your security guard about this letter. Or anyone else, for that matter. If you tell anyone, I will find out. And you and your mommy will be very, very sorry!

How will he find out? Is it even a he? I fan myself—not to cool off, but to give my shaking hands something to do. *How does this person know about the Regional Bee? Why would someone do this to me? A joke. It must be a joke. But jokes are supposed to be funny.*

Trembling, I shred the letter into tiny pieces, throw them into the toilet, and flush. I splash cool water on my face at the sink, fix my hair, and walk back to class as though nothing has changed.

But really, everything has.

23

Now, when I walk through the halls at school or sit in the lunchroom with Emma, I look around wondering who wrote that note and put it into my locker. *The custodian? The lunch lady? Coach Conner? He never liked me . . . or Mom. Or maybe it's the same person who's my secret admirer.* The thought makes me shiver.

I tell no one about the letter, even though I want more than anything in the world to tell Mom. I mean, how can someone find out if I whisper it to Mom in her bedroom late at night? Could the person have spies or have planted bugs? It seems unlikely, but I can't take that chance.

Mom's in real danger and I have to help. But the only way to save her is to ask her to drop out of the race. How can I do that? In a few days, four more states will hold their primaries, and Mom's expected to win three of them. How can

I ask her to quit now? But then again, how can I not? *Why is this happening to me?*

I carry all my textbooks with me all the time so I don't have to go to my locker anymore. They don't all fit in my backpack, and Mr. Martinez tells me he's sorry he can't help me hold them, but he's supposed to keep his hands free so he can do his job effectively.

I tell him it's okay. I don't tell him I'm glad he's nearby. But I am.

One day, Mrs. Durlofsky returns my diorama of *Romeo and Juliet*—the scene I created has Romeo on one knee pledging his love to Juliet, and Juliet tripping. There's no way I can carry all my textbooks and the diorama. I consider throwing out the diorama, but I want to bring it home and show Mom I do have a modicum (Modicum. M-O-D-I-C-U-M. Modicum.) of artistic ability. Besides, it will probably make her laugh.

Since I have no choice, I put my books on the floor, cradle my diorama in one arm, and face my locker. It's been so long that it takes me a while to remember the last number of my combination, but I do and the locker door swings open.

There is nothing inside . . . except for one white envelope lying at the bottom. I hold my breath and hope to see that familiar heart over the "a" in my name. *Maybe the other letter never really happened. Maybe I imagined it. Maybe . . .*

There are two words scrawled in red on the front of the

envelope: "Final Notice." I drop my diorama. Mr. Martinez rushes over. We both bend to pick it up and we knock heads. I rub my head and apologize profusely. And when I pick up my diorama, Juliet is broken.

"Great!"

While Mr. Martinez fumbles to fix Juliet for me, I grab the envelope from my locker and shove it between two textbooks. Then I throw my broken diorama into the trash can, grab my stuff, and run to my next class.

I keep the envelope pressed between my books until I get home.

Alone in my bedroom, I touch the envelope, but draw my hand back as though it's hot. "Final Notice." *What does that mean? And why does touching the envelope give me such a creepy feeling?*

I leave the envelope on my bed and go into my closet, reaching all the way to the back. I rub my fingers over the smooth wood of the box I keep there. It's heavy, weighted with memories. I press my nose to the wood and inhale. Sadly, the pine scent has diminished. I hug the box to my chest and whisper, "Daddy."

On my bed, I open the box and feelings flood through me. Happy feelings. Sad feelings. All mixed together inside this box.

I pull out my "Happy Bear-thday 8 Year Old!" card. It's just like the Valentine's Day card Emma gave me. *Emma, how I wish I could tell you what's going on!* I blink back tears and open the card from Daddy. Inside, it says in thick black letters: "I love you BEAR-y much!" *Did I realize how corny that sounds when I was eight?* In handwriting is: "So proud of you, Nessa. Love, Mom." And, in a sloppier, more relaxed script, "You're my big girl now. Love you, Nessy. Daddy."

I'd forgotten that my parents each signed my birthday cards. I kiss Daddy's signature, then put the card back in the box. Then I pull out the newspaper clipping about the plane and touch the black-and-white photo of the . . . I can't look at it. I push the article back into the box, grab the horrible envelope with "Final Notice" written on it, and shove that in, too. Then I slam the lid and push the box far back in the closet.

There's an ache in my chest, and I'm not sure if it's because I miss Dad or because I really wish Mom were here. Of course, she's off campaigning somewhere.

I sit at my desk in front of the computer. My hands shake as I compose the following e-mail:

Subject: Important Question
Hi, Mom,

    I've been giving this a lot of thought. I know it's important for you to become president. I know you've wanted it since you were ten. But why? Why is it so important?
    Vanessa

Later, Mom replies:

School assignment?

I e-mail:

> **No. Just for me. I want to know.**
> *I need to know.*

Mom sends the following e-mail:

> **Top Ten Reasons I Think I'll Make a Good President:**
>
> **10. I'll work to protect and preserve the environment—water, air, and land. Somebody's got to get mercury out of our water!**
> **9. I'll do my best to keep guns out of the hands of those who shouldn't have them. (This is most people.) Sometimes, Nessa, I think "NRA" (National Rifle Association) actually stands for "Nuts Running Amuck"!**
> **8. It's important to work on peace negotiations in the Middle East. We need to do all we can to stabilize that region.**
> **7. The poor need aid. Nessa, we don't realize how much we have in this country. So many people in this world do not have the basic necessities that we take for granted.**
> **6. I'd like to be part of the effort to bring the United States back to number one in education—especially science and math. Especially for girls!**
> **5. I will give tax breaks and incentives to the middle class for working hard and contributing to society. (I know, I sound like I'm campaigning here, but it's true.)**
> **4. I'd like to contribute to increased literacy worldwide.**

I'm a big believer in the Each One Teach One philosophy.
Reading is a key that unlocks many doors.

3. Here's a big one, Nessa: We need to stop our dependency
   on fossil fuels and fund alternative sources of cleaner energy. The reasons to work hard on this are too numer-
   ous to list here.

2. I'd like to see good-quality health care available for all
   Americans, especially our children and the elderly.
   But the number one reason I want to be president is:

1. I'd like to bring a feeling of hope and optimism back to the
   country so that Americans don't feel they need to sacrifice freedom for a sense of security and safety. Benjamin
   Franklin once wrote, "Those who would give up essential
   Liberty, to purchase a little temporary Safety, deserve
   neither Liberty nor Safety."

Whatever that means!
Mom sends one more e-mail:

> P.S. The real reason I want to be president is: If we lived
> in the White House, we could have midnight bowling parties
> right in our own home. How cool would that be?

I can't help laughing at that, but as far as the rest of
Mom's list, all I see is:

10. Blah.
 9. Blah.

8. Blah.

7. Blah.

6. Blah.

5. Blah.

4. Blah.

3. Blah.

2. Blah.

1. Benjamin Franklin once said, "Blah."

Because even though those things are really important, not one of them matters more to me than Mom's safety. And I'm willing to give up anything to ensure that. *But how?*

Two weeks later, near the end of March, when I watch the news to get a glimpse of Mom, I see a report about a man who's been killed in a plane crash. I bite the back of my hand to keep from crying. I imagine some girl having to go through what I went through. Maybe I can write her a letter of support. I sure got lots of them when it happened to us.

I reach into the back of my closet and pull out my Dad box again. I never make it to the letters of support, though. I pick up the article about the accident and read: "Charles Rothrock, attorney and husband of Florida governor Elyssa Rothrock, was killed in a plane crash early this morning. He was flying . . ." I wipe my nose with a tissue and kiss the clipping. "I love you, Daddy," I whisper. I put the article back and see the envelope with "Final Notice" scrawled in blood-red ink.

Since I'm already feeling brave from looking at the article, I slide my finger under the flap of the envelope. "Damn." The paper cut stings. Not a good sign. I hope there's no weird substance on the envelope that's now seeping into my bloodstream through the gaping wound. Actually, it's just a little slit below my knuckle, but it hurts like a gaping wound.

While sucking on the cut, I read:

Roses are red.
Violets are blue.

Maybe it's a poem from my secret admirer, after all. Maybe it has nothing to do with Mom or the campaign.

If your mom doesn't quit, VANESSA,
I shall kill you!
Or her.
So you'd better find a way to make her drop out. NOW!
And just a reminder: Tell anyone about this letter and you
can kiss your mommy good-bye. Forever!

My first thought? *Why did I wait so long to open this letter? What if Mom is in danger because I didn't do something right away?* My second thought? *That creep used my name again.* Third thought? No third thought. I grab the phone and dial Mom.

"Nessa. To what do I owe this honor?"

I have to tell her. But what if the phone line is tapped? Or what if the person who wrote the letters is standing right next to her?

"Nessa?"

"I'm here." My voice sounds crumbly.

"Everything okay?"

"Yes. No. I mean yes."

"Vanessa, put Grandma on."

"Grandma?"

"You know, the older woman who gave birth to me and gives you a large monetary gift every year on your birthday."

That's so not funny. Not now. I swallow hard. "Isn't Grandma campaigning with you?" *Is she in danger, too?*

I hear what I think is Mom hitting herself in the forehead with her hand. "I forgot," she says. "This schedule is crazy. Sometimes I don't even know what state I'm in. I mean, other than the state of confusion."

Still not funny, Mom.

"Who is there with you, Nessa?"

"Mrs. Perez, I guess. The usual people." I wonder if someone else might be in the house. Maybe the person who wrote the letters is in the house with me. I shake the thought from my mind and try to stop freaking myself out. "Who's there with you, Mom?"

"Some security personnel. Two assistants—Kyle James and Nicole Matthesen. Arnie, of course. Speaking of Arnie, guess who's signaling me to hang up? Nessa, are you sure you're okay?"

I'm afraid somebody's going to kill me. Or YOU! "I'm fine."
I've got to find a way to make Mom drop out of the race.

"Vanessa?"

"Yeah, Mom?" *I've got to come up with a plan.*

"I really need to go. Arnie's waving frantically. I think if I don't hurry, his arms are going to dislocate. Coming, Arnie! There, now he looks only mildly panicked. I think I'm late for a flight."

Oh, great. "Mom?"

"Yes?"

"Be careful."

"I'm always careful."

So was Daddy. "I love you."

"Nessa, I love you, too. I'll see you soon."

I hope so. I hold the phone awhile after Mom hangs up. Then I turn on the computer. When someone knocks on my door, I jump. "Come in."

It's Mr. Adams's assistant, Ms. Wright.

"Hi, Vanessa. Mr. Adams asked me to bring you these." She holds up a stack of envelopes. "Another pile of fan letters and an interview request."

"Okay." *Go away.*

"The interview request is from *Teen Scene Magazine*," she says, not getting my mental message.

Act normal, Vanessa. As if! "The *Teen Scene*"? I ask. "The *Teen Scene* with those gorgeous guys on the cover?"

She ducks her head. "I'll pretend I didn't hear that. But yes. In fact, it is the *Teen Scene* with a circulation of two and a half million. The editor in chief requested the interview with you. How could we say no?"

I bite my lip. "But kids, the ones who read that magazine, don't vote."

Ms. Wright grins. "Their parents do. And the kids will vote someday. Besides, any good press is, well, good press."

I shrug. "I guess so." *Please go away!*

"Be extra careful with your answers on that questionnaire. And be sure to give it back to our office for a final check."

I always give everything to your office for a final check. What else would I do? "Sure." I smile my sweetest smile, hoping she'll leave.

"Great, Vanessa. Thanks."

I nod, glad when she finally leaves the Purple Palace. I wish I could lock my door.

I ignore the pile of fan letters and the interview request from *Teen Scene Magazine* and get back to the computer. When Mrs. Perez calls me for dinner, I tell her I'm not hungry even though I'm starving.

When I find all the information I need, I e-mail the following message to Mom:

Subject: Ten Reasons You Should NOT Run for President

1. Andrew Jackson
2. Franklin D. Roosevelt
3. Harry S. Truman

4. Gerald Ford
5. Ronald Reagan, and more importantly,
6. Abraham Lincoln
7. James A. Garfield
8. William McKinley
9. John F. Kennedy, and most importantly,
10. I don't want YOUR name on this list!

I'm surprised when the phone rings minutes after I hit "send."

"Vanessa, why did you send this to me?" Mom sounds totally annoyed, but I'm relieved to hear her voice.

Isn't it obvious? "I just thought you should . . . be aware—"

"Vanessa, you know I'm very busy here. I thought we already went through this. Do you know what this list is?"

Of course I know what the list is. I sent it, didn't I? Be brave.
"Yes. Do you?"

Then, as though I hadn't just spoken, Mom says, "These are presidents who survived an assassination attempt. And those who didn't!"

"That's right," I say, glad she finally gets it, realizes how dangerous this is. Finally understands that she'll have to stop campaigning because nothing, and I mean nothing, is worth her life.

Mom sighs. "Nessa. Sweetheart. Listen to me: Nothing is going to happen to me. Do you understand? We cannot operate out of fear."

I take the rhomboid-shaped piece of purple cast from my

jewelry box—the part that says "To Vanessa, a courageous girl. Arnold Schwarzenegger." It smells like dirty socks, but I keep it anyway. *I'm not courageous. I'm scared. And I don't care that I'm operating out of fear.*

"Vanessa, I'm not going to let anything deter me from this campaign."

Not even a threat on your life? "Nothing?"

"Nothing."

"I was afraid of that," I mutter.

"What did you say? The connection's breaking up."

"It's just . . ." She doesn't understand at all. "I'll bet that's what those men on that list thought, too," I say in way too hysterical a voice, "before they were . . . they were . . ." I squeeze the phone. "Mom, you don't know. It could happen."

I thought I didn't want Mom to run for president for *me*—so I'd have more time with her. But I realize it's bigger than that. I don't want her to run for president for *her.* I don't want anything horrible to happen to her.

Her voice soothes my nerves. "Yes, it could happen, Vanessa, but it won't. I've got better protection than Fort Knox."

"Mom!"

"Sorry. But there really is security around me at all times. I'm safe."

You're never safe. I know that. "It can still happen. It did happen and I don't want it to happen again."

Mom lets out a big breath. "Daddy's . . . accident . . . was years ago. I realize that makes you depend on me more. But that just means I'll be more dependable."

My shoulders slump. "You sound like you're making a speech."

"Do I? Hazard of the job, I suppose."

How can she take this so lightly? I glance at the awful letter. *I have to make her understand.* "This is serious, Mom!"

"Lighten up, Nessa. Did you realize I have two things every person on that list doesn't?"

I think Mom is talking about me and maybe Grandma.

"Want to know what they are?"

I rub the piece of cast between my fingers. "I suppose."

"Boobs."

I laugh so hard I gag. "Mom!" I look around as though someone could have heard. "I can't believe you just said that."

"Well, I did. Now, get some rest, stop worrying, and I'll see you in a few days."

"A few days?"

"Vanessa, I'll be fine. Promise."

"So long, Mom," I say, reluctant to let her go.

"So long, Nessa."

After I hang up, I look at my Dad box. I wish he were here now. He'd know what to do. But Dad's not here. I pull my shoulders back. I have to find a way to save Mom, a way to get her to drop out of the race.

Because I'm not willing to have a Mom box, too.

24

By the time Mom returns home a few days later, I've talked myself into believing that the threatening letters are a hoax.

Someone from school, I'm convinced, is trying to scare me. And I feel like a complete idiot for falling for it. With my luck, it's Reginald. He might have dropped the secret-admirer letters into my locker and when that didn't get the kind of reaction he wanted from me, he moved on to scary letters. If Reginald is behind this, I hope he gets caught and ends up in huge trouble.

Actually, I hope it is Reginald. Or some kid from school playing a joke on me. A cruel joke. At least then Mom will be safe.

But in case the letters are real, especially the parts about not telling anyone, I still haven't told a single person.

As I sit in the Purple Palace with Carter in my lap, I reread the letter, lingering over its ridiculous rhyme. "Roses are red. Violets are blue." The more I look at it, the more I'm sure Mom will burst out laughing when she reads it and tell me it's even sillier than the one I showed her that day in her office with Governor Schwarzenegger.

But the icy shiver that runs along my spine when I touch the letter makes me think Mom may take this one seriously. The creepy feeling I get when I hold it makes me think it's real. And if that's the case, I shouldn't show Mom or anyone else because that would put Mom in terrible jeopardy.

I bite the skin beside my thumbnail and try to figure out what to do.

"I have to show Mom," I tell Carter, placing him gently on my pillow. "She'll know what to do."

I slip on my shoes, pray I'm making the right decision, and head out of the Purple Palace, gripping the letter in my sweaty, shaky hand. I almost turn back before I get to Mom's office, but take a deep breath and continue on.

When I stride past Ms. Purdy and her "Vanessa, don't—" into Mom's office, Governor Schwarzenegger is not there, which is a shame because he's a totally cool guy (even if he is a Republican).

Today, the lieutenant governor turns around and glares at me. She's not nearly as friendly as Governor Schwarzenegger. Maybe I don't have the best timing in the world, but this is a matter of life and death. I had to barge in on their—

"Vanessa, you're interrupting our budget meeting," Mom says coolly, anger in her eyes.

"But, Mom—"

"And you are never, ever to do this again. Do you understand?"

"Mom—"

"Walk out, please," she says in an even tone. "And make an appointment with Ms. Purdy to see me."

"An appointment?" *Thanks so much for embarrassing me in front of the lieutenant (Lieutenant. L-I-E-U-T-E-N-A-N-T. Lieutenant.) governor of Florida!*

Mom doesn't say another word. She raises her left eyebrow, and I turn toward the door and march out. *An appointment! To see my own mother.* File *that* under call-the-child-welfare-department!

Ms. Purdy loves that I have to make an appointment. She clucks her tongue at me no fewer than four times and draws out the process intolerably. Finally, she hands me a slip of paper that reads: "Dining room at seven."

Back in the Purple Palace, I grip Carter by his blue neck and say, "This is going too far! 'Dining room at seven.' I'm surprised she didn't write 'Formal attire required.' " I pace. "You know, Carter, this campaign is making Mom's head entirely too swelled. It's no wonder, too, with everyone catering to her every whim. 'Would you like more cream in your coffee, Governor?' 'Can I get you a pillow for your back, Governor?' Maybe one of her staff would like to wipe her nose for her, too!"

Carter says nothing.

"Dumb . . . donkey!"

At seven, when I join Mom in the dining room, she acts as if nothing is wrong. In fact, she's totally absorbed in some papers when I come in. To her credit, though, when she actually notices I'm there—it isn't hard to do because on the way in, I trip on a bump in the carpet—Mom removes her glasses, puts the papers in her briefcase, and says, "Hello, Nessa," in a really nice way.

Someone is serving our salads—"Governor, would you like fresh ground pepper on that?"—when Mom looks up and says, "Nessa, what was it you wanted to talk to me about earlier?"

I consider telling Mom it was nothing, but I have the letter on my lap. And the thought of keeping it from Mom any longer makes me feel sick to my stomach. I pull the letter from under my napkin and slide it across the table.

Mom slips on her glasses. "What's this?" she asks, not really looking at it yet. "Another fund-raiser from school?"

I mumble, "It's from school . . . sort of," and at that moment, Mom gasps. I'm afraid she'll choke on a radish, but she composes herself.

Letter clutched in her fist, Mom sputters, "Vanessa . . . how? Where?"

My heart pounds like crazy and my cheeks heat up. I guess I was hoping she'd tell me it was nothing to worry about. A prank. The look on her face scares me.

But I realize that Mom will want to drop out of the race now, and we can resume our regularly scheduled lives. And this creep will leave us alone, too. As long as he doesn't find out I showed Mom the letter. My heart pounds so hard my head hurts. But if Mom drops out quietly, he'll never find out I showed her the letter. This is the solution I was looking for all along. Now things will finally go back to normal. "I guess this is a credible threat, then?"

Mom shakes the letter at me. "This is . . . Where did you . . . ?"

"In my locker." *Calm down. You're freaking me out.* "At school."

"Your locker? At school?" Mom whips off her glasses and pushes back from the table. "Excuse me."

"Mom—"

She walks out, leaving her salad to wilt.

25

"Come here." Mom pats the edge of her bed. "Tell me about the letter."

It's been nearly two hours since Mom walked away from the dinner table. I've had plenty of time to think, er, panic about this situation. *Should I tell Mom everything?*

She fixes me with a stare. "Tell me everything Vanessa."

It's frightening when she does that. "This"—I swallow hard—"is the second letter."

"*What?*" Mom says.

I knew I shouldn't have told her everything.

"Vanessa! You have to show me these things right away. Do you understand? This is very . . . serious."

"But the letter said—"

"I don't care what the letter said. We've talked about this." Mom rubs the back of her neck. "You could have put yourself in terrible jeopardy by keeping this from me. When someone tells you not to tell, that's exactly when you should tell. Mr. Martinez is always with you at school. You should have—"

My sniffles stop Mom's tirade. She pulls me into her arms. "I'm sorry, Nessa. Don't cry. You must have been very scared by this."

I nod into her chest. *You have no idea how scared!*

She pulls back from me and wipes a tear from my cheek. "Nessa, it took a lot of courage for you to finally show me this letter. Thank you."

I nod again and wipe my nose with my sleeve.

Mom hands me a tissue. "Now, every detail you remember will be important for the Secret Service's investigation."

I gulp. "I don't know much. I . . ." A lump forms in my throat. *Mom's going to drop out of the race now. She'd never do anything that would put me in danger. And I feel awful about it.* "After I read the first letter, I got scared." Mom stares at me with such intensity I have to look away. "So I ripped it up"—I peek at Mom and whisper—"and flushed it down the toilet."

Mom closes her eyes. "Nessa."

"I'm sorry." *Sorry for disappointing you. Sorry for messing up your dream. Sorry. Sorry. Sorry!*

Tears stream down my cheeks, and Mom puts her arm around my shoulders. I feel her warm, damp breath on my ear and it tickles. "I'm so sorry for putting you in this situation," she says. "You'll be okay. This isn't your fault."

It is my fault, Mom. It's my fault you're going to drop out of the race now. And not because of those creepy letters. It's my fault because . . . I wished for it. First, I wanted you all to myself. Then I just wanted you to be safe. But either way, it's my fault.

"Nessa, there's only one thing we can do now," Mom says, squeezing my shoulders.

Why does she have to be so nice right before she tells me she's going to drop out of the race? "Mom—"

Mom's determined voice surprises me. "We're going to have to beef up security at your school."

I cough. "We're what?"

Mom stands and paces as she ticks off items on her fingers. "We'll have one security person stationed at your locker at all times. That way a note can be intercepted immediately, and we can catch this lunatic."

Aren't you dropping out of the race? My life is in jeopardy here. Not to mention your life. "Someone will be at my locker at all times?"

"Of course." Mom waves her hand. "And Mr. Martinez or other security personnel will be inside your classroom with you. Inside, not outside the door anymore. You will never be alone."

"Never be—?"

"The administration at your school has already been informed and, of course, as I said, the Secret Service will be working on this at their end."

"Mom?"

She stops and touches her finger to her chin. "And maybe we can—"

"Mom!"

She pulls her gaze away from the wall and focuses on me. "Yes, Vanessa?"

"Does this mean you're . . . you're not going to . . ."

"Not going to what? What more could I possibly do? If you've got any ideas, I'd love to hear them."

Drop out of the race. "Nothing."

26

As though I weren't enough of a dweeb at school! Now Mr. Martinez follows me *inside* every classroom. And there is a security guard stationed at my locker throughout the day. *What was Mom thinking?*

At least now I can go to my locker again. No one will drop anything in there with the Incredible Hulk standing nearby. The guard near my locker has forearms bigger than my thighs. He even scares me, and I'm *supposed* to be at my locker. *Note to self: Talk to Mom about the possibility of home-schooling.*

On the positive side, I no longer have to be humiliated that the Boob Fairy hasn't visited because I'm not allowed to change in the girls' locker room before or after P.E. anymore. If that's not a good thing, I don't know what is! I change in a stall in the girls' bathroom (after Mr. Martinez scopes it out), then leave my stuff in Coach Conner's office during

P.E. This also makes me late for class, which is wonderful because any minute not spent near Coach Conner is a minute well spent.

All the security makes me feel a little safer, albeit less approachable. Even Emma seems a little freaked out at lunch when Mr. Martinez stands right next to me instead of off to one side of the cafeteria. She's quieter than usual while we eat, but I don't feel much like talking anyway. Because, to tell the truth, even with all the security around me, I'm always alert, always paranoid that someone might try to do something horrible to me.

And no one on the staff at Lawndale Academy makes me more nervous than Coach Conner. Unfortunately, his class is mandatory.

"Rothrock, you need to work on upper-body strength," he shouts through a megaphone.

I'm a few yards off the floor, hanging on to a fat rope suspended from the ceiling. Sweat drips from my face, and my palms are raw. I look over and see Michael Dumas inch to the top of his rope, touch the beam near the ceiling, and shinny back down. I am shocked. *Maybe that boy's not the complete and total weakling he appears to be. Maybe—*

"Come on, Vanessa!" someone shouts from below. "We need our turns, too."

I hate P.E. I close my eyes and strain, but obviously, even without large mammary glands, my body's far too heavy to be supported by my scrawny biceps. (Biceps. B-I-C-E-P-S. Biceps.) I imagine the entire class staring up at my derriere and laughing. *P.E. should be outlawed as cruel and unusual punishment!* My arms shake and my left wrist aches. I consider letting go, but figure I'll miss the mat entirely and break my other wrist or smash my head and die instantly. I can almost see the headline in tomorrow's *Democrat:* GOVERNOR'S WEAKLING DAUGHTER DIES IN P.E. CLASS. FLORIDA ASHAMED!

"Upper-body strength, Rothrock!" Coach Conner shouts through his megaphone as though public humiliation will motivate me to try harder. "Upper-body!"

Upper-body? OHMYGOD! I'd cover my puny chest if my arms weren't busy with the rope. I'm entirely too embarrassed to come down now. I decide to hang on to the rope until class ends, but my uncooperative arms tremble so much that I shinny down, giving myself rope burns on unmentionable parts of my anatomy.

When I'm a couple of feet from the mat, I let go, stumble, and fall. As if I weren't already humiliated beyond belief! Guess who's standing there?

"You okay, Vanessa?" Michael Dumas holds his hand out to me. "You didn't hurt your wrist or anything, did you?"

When I take Michael's hand, my heart speeds up. "I'm okay. It's just—"

That's when I hear it. Murmurs from the other kids. "Dumb Ass." "Dumb Ass." "Dumb Ass."

I glare at Coach Conner. *Do something, you Neanderthal!* Coach actually grins. *I hate that man!* I make such tight fists that my fingernails bite into my palms. *Turn around,*

Vanessa. Tell them to shut up. Tell them it's pronounced "Doo-MAH," just the way Michael does. I let Michael's hand drop and scurry to the back of the girls' line.

I can't face Michael the rest of the period.

I'm still thinking about him and what a coward I am when I grab my backpack and clothes from Coach Conner's office. As I walk to the girls' bathroom, with Mr. Martinez a few feet behind, I thump myself in the forehead. *I should have stuck up for Michael.*

At the doorway to the bathroom, I stop and Mr. Martinez calls, "Anybody in there?" After a quick search, he nods and says, "All yours, Ms. Rothrock."

I choose the stall farthest from the door. After wiping my pits with my T-shirt, I slip into my regular clothes and bunch up my P.E. clothes to shove into my backpack. I notice an envelope sticking out from between my geometry textbook and my language arts textbook.

Mr. Martinez? I pluck the envelope out and open it. *Please let it be a love note. Or a note from one of my teachers. Or—* There are two sentences on the slip of paper.

Vanessa,
You can run, but you cannot hide.
July seems like a nice month to die.

"Ohmygod!" I scream.

"Ms. Rothrock?"

I hear Mr. Martinez's shoes pound into the bathroom.

The door to my stall flings open. I'm crouched there, shaking, the letter between my fingers.

"Are you hurt?"

I shake my head and hand him the letter.

He uses a piece of toilet paper to take it from me. "How . . . ?" he says, more to himself than to me. He reaches into his pocket and pulls out a clear plastic bag and drops the letter into it. He turns his head and says something into his shoulder.

"Mr. Martinez." My voice wobbles. "How did . . . ?"

He offers me his large hand, and I grab it, thinking of Michael offering me his skinny hand in P.E. "I don't know, Ms. Rothrock. But believe me, we will get to the bottom of this. Don't you worry."

I pick up my backpack and realize that only one person had access to it during P.E. It was lying exposed in his office. And the note said I can "run." *Could it be . . .*

"Ms. Rothrock, every avenue will be checked. Believe me, every individual will be investigated."

Coach Conner?

27

"Nessa, I told you," Mom says. "They did a complete background check on Coach Conner."

I press the phone to my ear and chew on the skin beside my thumbnail.

"You may not like him, but he has no record of any wrongdoing."

"That doesn't mean he didn't do *this*."

"No, it doesn't." Mom sounds exhausted. "Nonetheless, you're exempt from taking P.E. for the rest of the school year."

"Really?" I'm so excited, I squeeze Carter. I can't believe that all it took to get me out of P.E. was having my life threatened. Too bad there's only two and a half months left of school to enjoy that!

"You'll spend the period reading or doing homework in the library. Mrs. Foster suggested that."

"Okay." *Thank you, Mrs. Foster.*

"Nessa, I've got a lot of people working on this, but would you feel better staying out of school tomorrow?"

Did Mom just ask if I'd like to stay out of school tomorrow? "Well, I'd like to, but I have a math test and a language arts paper due."

"You're sure?"

I take a deep breath. "I'm sure. Mom?"

"Yes, sweetheart?" Her words are nice, but she sounds tired and edgy.

"That note said July is a nice month to die. What's in July?"

Mom doesn't answer right away. *Bad sign.* "It's nothing, Nessa."

I run everything through my mind—Grandma's birthday, Fourth of July, possibly a dignitary coming to town—but I come up blank. "Mom, I deserve to know."

She sighs. "The convention."

"What convention?"

"The Democratic National Convention takes place in July, Vanessa. That's where I'll officially be nominated to run for president."

"Oh." *I should have known that. I've got to start paying more attention to Mom's campaign.*

"It's one of the three biggest moments in a candidate's life. The first is the initial announcement, and the last consists of debates between the nominees of the offering parties. The convention is important."

"But you can't go," I say. "You'll just have to tell them you can't make it."

Mom laughs. "Not go? Vanessa, I'm going to be the headliner. The main attraction. And you're going to be there, too."

"Me?" I gulp. "I'm busy that day. When in July is it?"

"Vanessa, listen to me. I'll be there. You'll be there. Grandma will be there. It will be fine. In fact, it will be one of the greatest experiences of our lives."

My heart hammers "Mom?"

"Yes?"

"Never mind."

"You must have courage, Vanessa. Do you know what courage is?"

I roll my eyes and think of what Governor Schwarzenegger wrote on my cast. "It's when you're not afraid."

"Wrong. Courage is when you are afraid."

"It is?"

"Yes, it's when you're afraid, but you have the conviction to do what's right anyway."

"Mom, I think not putting yourself in harm's way *is* right."

"Not always."

"Huh?"

"Vanessa, what about a firefighter who runs into a burning building— Oh, for Pete's sake, Arnie, I'll be right there." Mom talks faster. "That firefighter puts himself in harm's way to rescue the baby."

"What baby?"

"The one in the burning building."

"There's a baby in a burning building?"

Mom clucks her tongue. "It doesn't matter. The point is, courage is the conviction to do what's right even though you're afraid."

I suddenly remember something. "Ohmygod!" I slap my hand to my mouth.

"What?"

"Mom: July."

"July? Honey, I told you not to worry. I need to go. Arnie looks like he's going to explode if I don't hang up."

"Mom, the note said, 'July seems like a nice month to die.' "

"Sweetheart, stop obsessing about that note. I told you the Secret Service is all over it."

"I know they are, but Mom . . ."

"Yes, Vanessa? What is it?"

"Daddy died in July."

28

I go online and look up the Democratic National Convention. Mom's right; it will be held in July, in Philadelphia, Pennsylvania. But Mom's wrong about her being the main attraction. Somebody else is going to have to do it. Because she's not going to be there. And neither am I.

None of us can go, as long as that creepy letter-writer is still out there. Right this very minute, he could be making plans to do something horrible to me and Mom at the convention. And I won't let that happen. I won't! If security can't keep someone from dropping a note into my backpack at school, how can they possibly keep some lunatic from hurting us at a giant venue like the Pennsylvania Convention Center in Philadelphia with thousands of people there? I've got to keep Mom—and me!—from going to that convention.

I reach for my desk calendar and flip past the pages for

April, May, and June. When I see "July," I gasp. *Why is this happening to us?* I rip out the page for July 1 and crumple it. I wish I could rip out all the pages for July and skip the month entirely. I tear out the pages for July 2 and 3, too. When I toss the crumpled pages into the trash can, I knock a pile of envelopes off my desk.

I lean forward to gather the envelopes, some of which have fallen under my desk. When I sit up, I bash the back of my head on the underside of my desk. *Could this day get any more painful?* As I rub the back of my head, I notice the interview request from *Teen Scene Magazine*. I pull out the page of questions and my heartbeat quickens. "Circulation of two and a half million." *That should be enough.*

I think I know exactly how to keep Mom from going to the convention in July. But I'll have to hurt her to do it. My shoulders slump. I put the page of questions on my desk and pull out a purple pen. I take a deep breath, but I can't make my fingers move. *How can I do this to Mom?*

I push the page out of the way and lay my head on my hands. "Oh, God, what should I do?" If I had a problem when I was younger, Mom was often in a meeting or away on business, so I went to Daddy. And anytime I told him I needed to talk, he closed the folders he was looking at and listened. He always said just the right thing and gave me a big hug after we were done talking.

I wish Daddy were here now, so much that my chest aches. I look around the Purple Palace, and my eyes settle on the closet door.

Even with Carter in the crook of my arm, my hand shakes as I reach into the back of the closet and pull out my Dad box. I carry it to my bed. This time, I open the lid, take a deep breath, and read the entire article. ". . . killed in a plane crash . . . just outside Pennsylvania. He left behind a daughter . . ." I run my fingers over the photo. *I'm what he left behind. Me. Vanessa Rothrock.* I read the date on the article: July 5. "Don't worry, Daddy." I kiss the photo. "I'll protect her."

I leave Carter on the bed, put away my Dad box, and read the *Teen Scene* interview questions. I think carefully about my answers, especially the last one. I scroll through my e-mails and copy part of one so that I'll get the answer just right.

I glare at Carter as I address a large envelope to the magazine's editor in chief. "I know I'm supposed to get this approved by the press secretary," I tell him. "But this is an emergency." I throw a dictionary at Carter. "Stop staring at me like that!"

I hang on to that envelope for nearly a week before I get up the courage to give it to someone to mail for me. I can't mail it myself because a staff member or security person might see me and intercept it. I get absolutely no privacy anymore. And if anyone from here reads it before it gets to the magazine, they'll tell Mom and my entire plan will be ruined.

On the last day of March, during lunch, I reach into my backpack to give Emma the envelope. But Mr. Martinez is standing right next to me. I can't take a chance he'll take it from me. Besides, I can't give the envelope to Emma. It says *"Teen Scene Magazine"* right on the front. Emma loves *Teen Scene;* she cuts out photos of the gorgeous guys from every issue and tapes them inside her locker door. I can't deal with Emma's questions about what I'm sending to *Teen Scene.* She'll probably want to *see* what I'm sending. And I can't let people know what I'm doing or they'll try to stop me.

It's bad enough that last night, when Grandma called to see how I was doing, I almost blurted the entire thing to her. Luckily I slammed my finger in a drawer just as I was about to spill the beans. And I was in entirely too much pain to say anything to Grandma other than "Ouch!" and "Love you" and "Good night."

The following day, the envelope is *still* in my backpack and I'm biting the skin beside my thumbnail, thinking about who would be the best person to ask to mail it for me.

Emma runs up to my locker, breathless. She puts her hands on my shoulders, and Mr. Martinez closes in. Emma steps back. "Guess who called me last night?" she whispers.

I tilt my head and think, *Reginald?* "No way."

Emma nods her head so hard I think it's going to fall off. "Yes. Reginald Trumball the Third called me last night. Me!"

"No!" I say again, shoving her. "Did he—ohmygod!— ask you out?"

"Better," she says, pulling her shoulders back.

"What's better than that?" Inside, I'm a mix of anger and

jealousy. Reginald is not a very nice person and Emma shouldn't go out with him. On the other hand, why didn't he ask *me* out?

Emma waves her hand at me. On her finger she's got this gorgeous gold ring with a little diamond on it.

Now I'm totally confused. "Reginald gave you *that?*"

Again, Emma nods furiously.

"Why would he—?"

Emma whispers hard in my ear, "Because he asked me to marry him."

"*What?* You're only in seventh grade."

"Well, I know. Not now." The corners of Emma's mouth turn up a little. "Later. You know, when we're older." The corners of her mouth turn up a lot. "And he wants to have at least seventeen children with me, too." She suddenly laughs so hard she spits on my forehead.

I wipe it off, take a big breath, and say, "It's April Fools' Day, isn't it?"

"Yeah!" Emma says, shoving me so hard I fall back into my locker.

Mr. Martinez steps forward and says in a deep voice, "Please don't do that."

Emma's face turns fifteen shades of red. She mouths the word "Sorry."

"Sorry," I echo her, embarrassed. Eager to change the subject, I ask, "So, where did you get that ring, anyway?"

Emma twists it off her finger and puts it in my palm. "My little brother won it at Chuck E. Cheese's. You can have it."

"Thanks." I shake my head. "I am so gullible."

"Yup."

"Reginald didn't really call you last night, right?"

Emma shakes her head at me. "What am I going to do with you, Vanessa Rothrock?"

"Uh—"

The bell rings.

"Happy April Fools' Day," Emma says.

"Yeah, right," I say, and head to Mr. Applebaum's room.

In advisory, I pass the envelope to Michael Dumas and ask him to put it in his mailbox for me when he gets home.

"Sure," he says, glancing at the address. "My sister Marigold loves this magazine. Did you write a story for them or something, Vanessa?"

"Something like that."

"Cool." Michael carefully slides the envelope into his backpack.

"Just make sure to mail it," I say before he can ask me why I don't mail it myself.

"I will," Michael says.

I glance up to make sure Mr. Applebaum isn't looking at us. He's bent over at his desk, scribbling something or other, completely oblivious to what I'm about to do to my mother. I get a pang in my chest. Then I remember that I'm doing it *for* her.

"Thanks, Michael." I open a book on my desk, then turn back to Michael. "Make sure you mail it."

"Okay."

"Today."

He raises an eyebrow and his eyelid doesn't twitch even once. Michael has been dressing much better, too, since he got his contact lenses. "Vanessa," he says, "I promise I'll mail it as soon as I get home. Okay?"

"Thanks. That's great, Michael." *Is it?*

29

"*Teen Scene Magazine?*"

It's been two months since I gave Michael the envelope to mail. To be honest, with all the craziness of the campaign and worrying about the stalker who gave me those letters and talking Emma out of telling Reginald that she adores him and studying for final exams, I hadn't thought much about the questionnaire I had sent to *Teen Scene*.

As the last wisps of my dream slip away, Mom's voice comes through loud and clear. "The damned *Teen Scene*, Vanessa! With a circulation of two and a half million."

I pull the comforter from my face, open one eye, and peer over Carter's donkey ears. I see Mom and my heart soars. She said she'd be home Saturday and she is. But she's clutching a rolled-up magazine and her cheeks are bright red.

I sit up and open the other eye, squeezing Carter to me. "Mom?"

"Why, Vanessa?" Mom smacks the magazine into her palm, and I get the feeling she wishes she were smacking me. "Why?"

Why what? OHMYGOD! "Mom," I say, my voice gravelly, "I just answered the questions they asked and sent it in."

Mom smirks. "Then you *did* do this! I was hoping it was a mistake. I was hoping—"

"Mom, I didn't—"

"No, Vanessa! You didn't mean to do anything wrong, but you didn't send your answers through the press secretary's office like you were supposed to." She smacks the rolled-up magazine into her palm again so hard I'm sure it stings. "Standard procedure and you know it! Do you have any idea—?"

"But . . ." *I was trying to save you.*

"But nothing. You wrote something I sent you in a private e-mail, something that was intended for your eyes only, and unfortunately they had no compunction about printing it!"

Compunction. C-o-m-p-u—

"Vanessa, are you listening to me?"

"I'm sorry." *n-c-t-i-o-n. Compunction.* "Yes, of course I'm listening."

" 'Sorry' isn't going to cut it this time."

I did this for you. To keep you safe.

"You really outdid yourself."

I did it for you, Mom!

"The opposition is going to have a field day with this one." Mom paces, then gets so close to my face I can smell coffee on her breath. "Are you happy now, Vanessa? You'll finally get your wish. They'll bury me with this."

Bury you? "Stop!"

"Stop? You want me to stop, Vanessa?" I feel Mom's warm breath on my cheek, but I don't move. "Do you have any idea what you did by sending that unapproved response in? If you thought you were being funny—"

"Funny?"

"Yes, did you think it was funny to write that I thought 'NRA' really stood for 'Nuts Running Amuck'?"

"You did e-mail that to me," I say quietly.

"What did you say?" Mom snaps.

"Nothing!" *I saved your life. Even if I did ruin your chances of becoming president.*

Mom hurls the magazine to the floor. "Your little stunt has probably cost me the election." Hands on hips, she turns her back to me.

I'm so mad, I fling Carter at her. He misses and hits the door. "I was trying to help. Don't you get that? I was trying to help!"

"Help?" Mom shrieks, and whirls around toward me. "Help? You call that helping? Oh, I'd hate to see what you'd do if you were trying to hurt me, Vanessa."

I make a fist with my right hand and scream, "You just don't get it!"

Mom points at me. "No, Vanessa. You don't get it. YOU

don't get it. Because of what you did, I'll have to work even longer hours trying to repair the damage you've done. I'll have to meet with high-ranking members of the NRA and apologize again and again and again." Mom takes a breath through gritted teeth. "I'll be away from you even more often. Now do you get it?"

I push past her, rush into my bathroom, slam the door, and scream, "Yeah, I get it!" Then I lock the door and lean my back against it. Security be damned!

30

Mom spends days on the road counteracting what her opponents have dubbed Nutgate. She apologizes to the president of the NRA, but he doesn't buy it. On TV and in newspapers, she has to assure everyone that she does believe in the Constitution and the right to bear arms. It's painful to watch.

A week after Nutgate breaks, Emma pulls me into the girls' bathroom. We go into the last stall and whisper to each other so that Mr. Martinez can't hear what we're saying.

"It's terrible," I say to Emma.

"I know."

"I'm totally embarrassed all the time."

"Me too."

I look up at Emma. Her eyes and nose are red. I can't imagine why she's that upset about my problems with my mother. "Are we talking about the same thing? About me sending in that awful questionnaire to *Teen Scene* and totally ruining my mom's life?"

Emma shakes her head no and peeps, "Worse."

"Worse?" I can't imagine what could be worse than your own mother hating you and everyone on her staff glaring at you every time you walk by because of all the extra hours they have to put in for "damage control."

"It's about Reginald," Emma says.

I squeeze my eyes closed, then look at Emma. "You didn't?"

She nods.

"When?"

"Just now. Before lunch."

Tears drip down Emma's freckled cheeks, and I hug her. "What happened?"

Emma pulls back and wipes her nose with a square of toilet paper. "I got up my courage."

"Yes?"

"And I went to Reginald at his locker."

"Yes?"

"And I—" Emma bursts into a fresh round of tears. I give her a length of toilet paper and wait till she's ready. "And I said, 'Reginald, I was wondering if you'd like to go out to the movies with me this weekend.' " Emma's shoulders bob up and down.

"What did he say?"

"Nothing."

I step back and bang into the stall door. "Ouch. You

mean you poured your heart and soul out to that boy and he said absolutely nothing?"

Emma sniffs. "He laughed."

"What!" I feel blood rush up my neck and heat my face to a boiling point. "He laughed!"

Emma nods. "He laughed, then he walked away."

"Oh, Emma." I hug her again. "You are way too good for that boy."

We wait until the last possible moment, when Emma's face is nearly back to its normal color, to leave the bathroom and head to our classes. Mr. Martinez only called in to check on us twice. And, I suppose, he kept other girls from coming in and using the bathroom while we were in there. So there are some advantages to having a security guard.

Between Emma's disaster with Reginald—that boy is just plain mean—and my debacle with Mom, I can't concentrate and totally bomb on my English exam. My last final exam of my seventh-grade year and I blow it. I hope someday Mrs. Durlofsky will forgive me.

On one hand, I'm glad to get home and be done with school for the day—my penultimate (Penultimate. P-E-N-U-L-T-I-M-A-T-E. Penultimate.) day, the next-to-last day of the school year. On the other hand, I'd rather not face being home, because Mom comes back from wherever she was today, and I still haven't said I'm sorry. I know I had a really good reason for doing what I did, but Mom's life has been miserable ever since *Teen Scene* printed her comment about the NRA.

I guess, all things considered, I shouldn't have done it, because Mom didn't drop out of the race. And as far as I know, they still haven't caught the person who dropped those threatening letters into my locker and backpack.

As I walk into the kitchen, I sigh, and I wonder how my life got so complicated. At least school will be over tomorrow and that's one less thing to worry about, but unfortunately, that also brings me one day closer to dealing with July. I keep hoping they'll catch that lunatic before the convention.

I'm happy to see a lemon square on a plate. The sweet and sour scents make me feel a little better, and I enjoy one warm, chewy bite before I notice the note.

Nessa,
Welcome home. Enjoy your snack, then come to my office as soon as you're done.
Mom

Is she still furious with me? I can't tell from the note. She didn't write "Love, Mom." But she did write "Welcome home." My stomach gets tense, and I can't eat any more of my lemon square. Everyone in Mom's office must hate me, especially her secretary, Ms. Purdy. I spend a full five minutes stewing about this before I walk to Mom's office.

"Hello, Vanessa. Nice to see you."

"Hi," I say cautiously. *Why is Ms. Purdy being nice to me?*

"And how are we today?" she asks.

You might be fine, Ms. Purdy, but I'm pretty sure Mom still hates me and I have no idea why she called me down here. There's a crazy person planning to kill me or Mom next month! Oh, and the Boob Fairy has snubbed me entirely. "Fine, Ms. Purdy. And you?"

"Thank you for asking," she says, pulling a photo from her drawer and passing it across the desk to me. "Next week my granddaughter is going to spend a week with me. I'm taking her to Disney."

"She's adorable."

"Isn't she, though?" She looks up. "Your mother said tomorrow is your last day of school."

Mom remembered? "Yes, it is."

"Good luck."

"Thanks."

Ms. Purdy glances at the clock on her desk, then makes a phone call. "Your mother will see you now."

As soon as I walk into her office, Mom nods at the chair across from her, and I slide in silently. *I'm sitting in the same chair that Governor Schwarzenegger sat in.*

Mom links her fingers. "The good news?"

There's good news? "Yes?"

"My numbers are up seven to ten points, depending on which poll you look at."

"That's great news. Right?"

"The bad news?"

There's bad news? I swallow and whisper, "Yes?"

"Because of Nutgate, as the press so glibly dubbed it, my numbers had originally dropped over fifteen points."

"Oh. Mom, I'm sorry." Even though I feel really bad, finally apologizing to Mom makes me feel lighter somehow. "I'm really sorry." *You have no idea how sorry. It seems like ever since that happened everyone has been glaring at me, even Mr. Applebaum.*

Mom leans back in her chair. "I know you're sorry, baby."

I smile because Mom used Daddy's nickname for me.

"There is something you can do to help."

I lean forward. "You want me? To help? You?" I realize I sound like Cro-Magnon Woman.

Mom nods, and the door to her office opens. "Right on time," she says.

I twist around and see Mr. Adams and his assistant, Ms. Wright. I cannot look at them. I know they hate me for sending in that awful interview sheet without getting their approval.

"Vanessa?" Mr. Adams says.

I force myself to look at him. "Yes, sir?"

"We have work to do."

I look at Mom.

"Sorry, I haven't had a chance to tell her yet," she says.

Mr. Adams says, "That's okay. I'll—"

"Mr. Adams," I blurt, "before we start, I just want to say . . ." I feel everyone's eyes boring holes through me. "I just want to say I'm sorry I sent in that questionnaire without giving it to you first." I look at my lap. "Really sorry."

"Vanessa." He leans toward me. "You might need to apologize to my wife and kids. They haven't seen much of me these last couple of weeks while I've been doing damage control for your mother."

"I will."

Everyone laughs.

"I'm kidding." He runs his fingers through his short gray hair. "Sort of. But let's move past that and on to the next thing. Always look forward." He glances at Mom, and she nods. "The Democratic National Convention is next month, Vanessa."

I wince, and Mom gives me one of those don't-start-that-again looks.

"Yes," I say to Mr. Adams. I'm trying to control the panic rising in my throat.

"And we need to start rehearsing your part."

I choke on my own saliva. "My . . . part?"

"It's not what you're thinking," Mom says. "No speeches or anything."

"Speeches?"

"But it's still important," Mr. Adams says. "You're going up onstage after your mother's speech. She'll raise your arm in victory. Then you'll smile and wave with your other hand." He demonstrates.

I feel blood drain from my face. "Smile. Wave."

"It's not quite as easy as it sounds," Mr. Adams says. "But we can't mess this up, Vanessa. There's no room for . . ."

Tripping?

". . . error."

Ms. Wright leans forward and talks fast. "You can't walk up too early. Or late. We'll have a signal. A phrase your mother will say. And you must smile, Vanessa. Smile as though it's the best moment of your life."

"What if—?"

"Smiling is very important," Ms. Wright says. "Crucial, really. We'll have your teeth whitened right before the convention and—"

"What if I trip?"

Mom gasps. She must not have thought of that.

Mr. Adams puts up his hands. "You won't, Vanessa. It's as simple as that. We'll meet with you. You'll practice, practice, practice and you *will not trip*."

Ms. Wright continues, "Someone will choose your attire."

"My attire?"

"Of course, Vanessa. Don't worry about a thing. The staff will make sure you're fully prepared."

Prepared for what? As Ms. Wright drones on, all I can think about is the last line of that note: *July seems like a nice month to die.*

31

Emma and I meet at my locker and exchange yearbooks. I turn to the blank back page and write:

Dear Emma,

    It's been great. Thank you for being such an awesome friend. Next year, at the spelling bee, wouldn't it be cool if we could both go all the way?

    Love,

    Vanessa

OHMYGOD! Did I really just write *that* in my best friend's yearbook? It's not like I can erase it or cross it out.

We switch back.

"Mine's stupid," I say.

"Mine's stupid," Emma says, and we both laugh.

I turn to the back page to read what she wrote.

Dear Vanessa,

    It's been great knowing you over the years. I don't know what I would have done without you this year. You know what I mean.

    Thanks for everything.

    BFF,

    Emma

And she drew her best picture of a ladybug ever.

We hug and talk about all the things we'll do together over the summer no matter how busy Mom's schedule is. Emma says anytime I want I can sleep over her house to get away from it all.

All I can think is *That sounds great, but we'd better squeeze all that stuff in before July.* I don't tell Emma about that, though. I've already caused enough trouble for Mom.

Emma and I make a plan to meet later, and she heads toward her class.

I check to make sure my locker is completely empty and happily slam it closed for the last time this school year. I'm squeezing my yearbook to my puny chest and thinking about who else I want to sign it when I hear a whimper.

Mr. Martinez holds up a hand and peers around the corner.

I tiptoe behind him.

Another whimper comes from someone being blocked by the gargantuan security guard who watches my locker. The guard's back is to us.

I gasp and drop my yearbook. It makes a loud thud on the floor, but the security guard doesn't turn toward the sound. *Have they caught the guy? Can I finally stop worrying?* I can't see who the guard has pressed against the wall because his hulking frame completely blocks my view of the other person.

"Give it to me," the guard barks.

Again, the whimpering, like a puppy whose paw has been stepped on.

Mr. Martinez turns to me. "Agent Lansky's got this covered. Let's get you to class."

I see a foot peek out from behind the guard. *Whose sneaker is that?*

"I . . . I . . . don't need to get to class," I say. *Technically not a lie, since it is the last day of school.* I strain to get closer, but Mr. Martinez blocks the way.

"What's going on?"

I reel around. "Reginald. It's . . . it's . . ." I point to the guard. "He has someone."

"Cool," Reginald says, craning his neck. "Who is it? What'd he do?"

Reginald's voice annoys me. I think of what he did to Emma, and I want to stomp on his foot. More kids gather behind us. I ignore Reginald and turn back to the situation.

The guard steps back. "Listen, kid—"

"Ohmygod!"

Michael Dumas, shivering, is pressed against the wall, one arm behind his back.

"It's nothing. It's nothing," Michael says in a voice much too high-pitched for a guy his age.

Mr. Martinez grips my shoulder. "Ms. Rothrock, we really must—"

"One minute." I don't budge.

"Give me the letter, kid," the guard growls.

Michael shakes his head.

"Now!"

I flinch.

Michael's eyelid twitches, but he looks at the guard. "No. It's mine."

Go, Michael!

"Then why were you slipping it into Ms. Rothrock's locker?"

I gasp. *Michael isn't . . . He couldn't be . . .*

Michael squeezes his eyelids closed. I don't know if he's trying to stop the twitch or if he wishes he could disappear.

"We'd better go," Mr. Martinez whispers in my ear. "You don't need to see this."

I think of Michael's butterfly touch on my hand the day I broke my wrist. I remember him offering me his hand when I fell off the rope in P.E. "Please, Mr. Martinez," I whisper. "Please."

Mr. Martinez lets out a breath and shakes his head. "Okay. Stand next to me. Don't move any closer to the situation."

Thank you. I nod. *It can't be Michael who wrote those horrible letters. It can't be.*

"This is your last chance, kid," barks the guard.

"No," Michael says, his lips pressed tight.

"You tell him, Dumb Ass!"

I whirl around and face Reginald. There are dozens of kids around us now. I glimpse Emma at the back of the crowd, trying to push her way forward.

"What?" Reginald asks me, laughing. "What'd I do?"

I remember how I felt when Reginald read my list of deficiencies. I think of all the times he teased Michael about his name. I remember how he laughed when Emma asked him to go to the movies.

Then I hear Michael whimper again, and my chest fills with rage. "Reginald Trumball, you are a nasty and despicable person."

Reginald grins and touches his hand to his chest as if to say, "Who, me?"

"Yes, you!" I shove him.

He stumbles backward.

"Watch out!" Holly Stevens squeals, pushing him away. "New shoes here!"

I feel Mr. Martinez squeeze my shoulder, and I shrug his hand off. "Look, Reginald," I say, painfully aware that kids are staring, "it's pronounced Doo-MAH."

"Huh?" He rakes a hand through his wavy hair.

"Let me spell it out for you: Michael's last name is Doo-MAH. D-u-m-a-s." I'm breathing hard. "And that's what you're going to call him from now on."

"Go, Vanessa!" someone yells. I think it's Emma.

"That's what I said." Reginald looks at the kids surrounding us and smirks. "Dumb Ass!"

I get in Reginald's face, not even caring that I ate onions in my omelet this morning, and yell. "You're the dumb ass, Reginald!"

Kids laugh and hoot, and I feel pretty good until, suddenly, everyone falls silent. I hear only one voice.

"Ms. Rothrock!"

OHMYGOD! I squeeze my eyelids. When I open them, Mrs. Foster is standing in front of me with her hands on her hips. "Young *lady?*"

I look toward Mr. Martinez, but he just stands there. *Thanks for nothing.*

"I'm sorry, Mrs. Foster. It's—it's just—" I stammer.

"NO!" Michael screams.

I turn in time to see the hulking guard pluck an envelope from Michael's fingers.

My hand flies to my mouth. *It was Michael!*

"Oh, what now?" Mrs. Foster snaps. "Rothrock, don't move."

How could Michael do such a thing? How could he?

"There's nothing to see here," Mrs. Foster says to the crowd of kids and a few teachers. "Go to your classes."

No one moves.

She claps three times. "Now."

Still, no one moves.

Mrs. Foster screeches, "I don't care if it is the last day of school. Go to your classes now or each one of you will stay after school for a three-hour detention. With me!"

They scatter.

Mrs. Foster didn't need to tell me not to move. My feet are granite. But my legs feel like the soft part of Mrs. Perez's lemon squares, and I'm not sure they're going to support me.

The guard holds the envelope with one hand while pressing Michael to the wall with his other.

"Give it back," Michael says, reaching feebly.

"I'll take that, sir!" Mrs. Foster says, plucking the envelope from the guard's fingers.

He lets go of Michael, who looks like he might crumble.

"Ma'am!" the guard says. "I need that. It's evidence." He reaches for the envelope, but Mrs. Foster holds her arm high so he can't reach it.

"That's one tough lady," Mr. Martinez mutters.

"Ma'am," the guard says again. "This is official government business. I insist that you hand that envelope to me." He reaches for it again.

Mrs. Foster steps back and keeps it just out of his reach. "Young man, this boy is a student in my school. My school. And if he's doing something inappropriate in my school, I, not you, will be the first to know." She pulls her shoulders back and faces Michael. "Mr. Dumas, please tell me what this is about."

Michael's mouth moves but no words come out.

"Well, I'll find out for myself, won't I?" And in one swift motion, Mrs. Foster rips open the envelope.

"Ma'am!" the guard says.

"Ohhh!" Michael moans.

Mrs. Foster turns her back to the guard, holds the card far in front of her face, and reads in a clear, strong voice: "Shall I compare thee to a summer's day?"

"No," Michael whispers. "Please. No."

Mrs. Foster looks at Michael and smiles, but he can't see this because his eyes are closed and he's shaking his head.

"Why," she says, "this is from Shakespeare." She glares at the guard. "A student quoting from Shakespeare doesn't sound very troubling to me."

That's when Michael opens his eyes. I've never seen his eyelid twitch this much. His lower jaw is dangling and he's shaking his head as Mrs. Foster flips open the card.

She clears her throat and reads, "Vanessa, thou art hot!" Her lips twist and she mumbles the rest to herself.

The first sound I hear is Mr. Martinez stifling a laugh.

The second sound is a strange gurgling from Michael.

Mrs. Foster grabs Michael's elbow. "Michael Dumas, what on earth were you thinking? Do you not know that Ms. Rothrock is the governor's . . . the governor's . . . Wait until your parents hear about this!"

Michael moans.

As Mrs. Foster drags Michael past us, he looks in my eyes and mouths the words "I'm sorry."

You're sorry? Oh, Michael.

I glare at the guard who had been pinning him against the wall, grab my yearbook from the floor, turn, and walk to class. Mr. Martinez follows. I know I should feel bad about what's going to happen to Michael in Mrs. Foster's office. I know I should feel totally relieved that Michael is not the person who wrote those horrible, threatening letters. I should probably even feel a little proud of myself for what I finally said to Reginald. But what's really on my mind is that Michael Dumas is my heart-above-the-"a," sweet-poems-in-my-locker, not-so-secret admirer.

And the best part—just thinking about it makes the skin on my neck tingle—Michael Dumas thinks I'm hot!

32

"Michael?" I press the phone to my ear and push Carter down into the side of my suitcase.

"Vanessa?"

Michael sounds surprised. He's sounded surprised each time I've called since school ended. It makes me feel good.

"What's up, Michael?"

"Nothing much. What are you doing?"

I lay my purple pajamas in the suitcase. "Packing."

"You leave tomorrow, right?"

I sigh and sit on my bed. "Actually, I'm leaving today. Grandma is taking me sightseeing before the convention." The word "convention" sends goose pimples along my neck and arms. "She said if I'm the daughter of the soon-to-be president, I must visit the Liberty Bell, Independence Hall, and the National Constitution Center."

"We did that. My parents took us all around Philadelphia last summer," Michael says. "It's a cool city. Except it's a hot city in July."

As though I don't have enough to worry about. Now my hair's going to frizz from the heat!

"You ready for your part, Vanessa? Smile. Wave. Smile. Wave."

I hunch over. "Michael, to tell the truth I'm a little scared." *A lot scared. But not just about getting on the stage.*

"Oh, Vanessa, you'll do great. You'll be the best smiler and waver that convention ever saw. I wish I were going with you. I mean . . ." Michael coughs.

"Me too." *Did I just say that?*

"You do?"

"Sure, Michael. We could check out all those historic places together."

"Yeah, that would be fun. But I'm going to be in North Carolina with my parents, remember?"

"Oh, yeah. Are you going to be able to watch the convention on TV?" I hit myself in the forehead with the heel of my hand. *As if a normal kid would actually watch all that political stuff on TV while he's on vacation and there are other perfectly good shows to watch.*

"I'll watch the whole thing," Michael says, "especially the part when you'll be onstage."

I blush so hard, I grab Carter from my suitcase and fan my face with him. "I'll tug my ear."

"You'll tug your *beard*?"

"My *ear*. That will be our secret signal. It will mean I'm saying hello to you."

"That's nice. And Vanessa?"

"Yes?"

"Thanks again for sticking up for me that day in the hall. You know, with Reginald and all. I heard what you said to him."

Reginald! I can't believe I ever liked that boy. He's got a nice-looking package, but there's nothing inside. "You're welcome. Thank you for"—I think of the sweet poems dropped in my locker—"um, everything."

"I can't believe that card I wrote you. It was so . . ."

Sweet. Flattering.

". . . embarrassing! I'm sorry again about that."

I'm not.

"It was really dumb. I'm just glad it was the last day of school or Foster probably would have suspended me for a week. It was bad enough when she called my mom and I had to read her what I wrote."

"Hey, if anyone knows about being embarrassed, Michael, it's me. I'm the Queen of Embarrassment!"

"You?"

"Definitely. I'm sure you've noticed."

"Vanessa, you're like the most perfect person I know."

My face gets so hot my ears tingle. "Um, thanks."

"Coming, Mom!" Michael yells. "Sorry, Vanessa, I've got to go. They're ready to leave."

"Tell Marigold I wish her luck at her academic camp. And have fun in North Carolina."

"Yeah, sure. Vanessa?"

"Umm?"

"Have fun at the convention. Good luck onstage and all. Break a leg."

I gulp.

"Just not a wrist. Ha ha."

I try to laugh, but all that comes out is a weird gurgle.

"You all right, Vanessa?"

July seems like nice month to . . . "Yeah, Michael. I'm fine."

"Well, have a great time in Philadelphia. You're so lucky."

"Lucky?"

"Be right there, Mom!" Michael yells. Then, more quietly: "I promise I'll watch you on TV. Hey, maybe we can go bowling or something when you get back."

If I get back. "Sure, Michael. That would be nice."

33

My chair is less comfortable than I had imagined it would be. I shift from butt cheek to butt cheek, trying to keep either side from falling asleep. "It's loud in here," I shout to Grandma, who's seated to my right.

"Shush, Vanessa," she says, not looking at me. Her hands are in her lap, and she's totally focused on the speaker at the podium.

I shush, but no one could have heard me anyway, it's so noisy in the gigantic hall. Even though a United States senator is giving a passionate speech onstage, most people continue their personal conversations as though he isn't even speaking. How rude! They'd better pipe down when Mom is introduced. She's been practicing her acceptance speech for weeks.

Mom's running mate, vice presidential candidate Senator Miller, gave his speech last night. He looked very, um, vice presidential. And between sightseeing excursions in Philadelphia—it *is* a cool city—these past few days, Grandma and I listened to some of the other speakers: governors, senators, and a former president. It's pretty cool that with all those famous people giving speeches, Mom's speech tonight is the main attraction. *Mom!*

I look around for suspicious people. All I see, though, are policemen and policewomen and lots of people in dark suits who must be Secret Service agents. Mom's right. She is protected better than Fort Knox. I allow my shoulders to relax a little, and I give my ear a tug in case Michael is watching on TV.

Grandma yanks my arm. "Hands in lap. Pay attention, dear. The senator is speaking."

I'm fully aware that the senator is speaking because I'm looking at his face on a giant screen behind him. I mean, the screen is so enormous that just one of his teeth is the size of the *Oxford English Dictionary.*

Soon he'll finish his speech and introduce Mom. Then, when she's done, Grandma and I will join her onstage. *Smile. Wave. Smile. Wave. Don't trip. Smile. Wave. Smile. Wave.*

OHMYGOD! I can't go onstage after Mom's speech because then I'll appear on that giant screen, too. If I have a pimple—which I do, on the side of my nose!—it will look like Mount Vesuvius. "I can't do this."

"Shhh," Grandma whispers.

I shrink down in my rock-hard chair, only to have

Grandma poke me and demonstrate how to sit tall. I pull my shoulders back the way Ms. Wright showed me about a million times; then I turn toward the delegates in the audience. Someone waves a sign that reads: "Texas for Rothrock." Another person holds one that reads: "AFL/CIO for Rothrock." Then I see someone dancing around with a bumper sticker—the same one I put on my bed and my computer and my closet door. It reads: Rothrock and Miller—Hope for a Better America."

It's so cool that all these people love Mom. *Daddy should be here. He would have loved this.* Just thinking of Daddy fills me with peace. *Maybe there's nothing to worry about.* I look at the police officers and Secret Service agents again. I mean, it's not like anyone could possibly get to me or Mom with all these people here to protect us.

I wish Emma were sitting beside me. She'd love all this excitement, but she's at an equestrian (Equestrian. E-Q-U-E-S-T-R-I-A-N. Equestrian.) camp in Connecticut this week. It would be cool if Michael had been allowed to come with us instead of having to go with his family to North Carolina. *Michael!* I haven't tugged on my ear in at least three minutes. Tug. Tug. *Hello, Michael.* Tug. Tug.

"Vanes—"

"It is my great privilege to introduce to you . . ."

Grandma pinches my arm so hard tears spring to my eyes. I nod and put my hands in my lap.

". . . the *woman* who will surely become the next

president of the United States of America." Then the senator shouts: "Elyssa. Victoria. Rothrock!"

The room erupts as though a rock star's name had just been announced. There's a hurricane of cheering and clapping and stomping, and my chest swells with pride. *How could I ever have wanted Mom to drop out of the race?* Grandma yanks my elbow, and we're standing and clapping and stomping, too. I'd put my fingers in my mouth and whistle for Mom if I weren't afraid Grandma would pinch me again. That hurt.

As Mom strides across the stage, she's all smiles and self-confidence. Talk about grace under pressure! She hugs the senator, nods, and steps up to the podium. On the giant screen behind her, Mom's face is two stories high. Thank God that woman has good pores.

I look at Grandma. She's beaming and clapping so hard I'm sure her hands will still be sore in the morning.

Up on the stage, Mom speaks. "Thank you. I'm—" She waits, grinning. "I can't tell you how much—" She has to start half a dozen times because the applause doesn't stop. People are on their feet, screaming and whistling and waving signs. I feel my chest vibrate from the noise.

Amazed, I look around at the mass of people again. Toward the center, several rows back, I notice one man sitting, hunched over. *Why is he sitting when everyone else is standing and clapping?* I squint, but all I can see is the top of his dark hair. Even from that view, he looks vaguely familiar.

I face forward and continue smiling and clapping for Mom, but a nervous feeling runs through me. Police are stationed a few feet apart in front of the stage, facing the audience. *Stop worrying, Vanessa.*

Stop worrying? Even if everything goes exactly as planned, as soon as Mom finishes her speech, I have to get onstage. I'll be on that giant screen!

In an effort to stop thinking about it, I focus on what Mom's saying.

"Let's look toward the future with hope. Let's look toward the future with optimism. Let's do these things for our children and our children's children."

Even though a lot of people have taken their seats now, applause breaks out again. *If people keep interrupting Mom's speech with applause, it will take hours for her to finish. Good. I really don't want to get up on that stage.*

I glance toward the guy several rows back who was sitting when everyone else was standing. I'm shocked to see he's staring directly at me. And he's wearing . . . a . . . a . . . bow tie! *Mr. Applebaum? What is my math teacher doing at the Democratic National Convention?*

My heart thunders and I feel my cheeks heat up. *He's probably just a fan of Mom's, although he never mentioned it in class. Even if he is a fan, why would he fly all the way to Philadelphia when he could just watch her on TV? Maybe he's a delegate for Florida and he's supposed to be here. Maybe—*

"My vision for America is one of hope and prosperity. My vision for America is one of compassion."

Maybe it isn't Mr. Applebaum at all. I mean, what are the chances that my math teacher flew all the way to the convention just to see Mom in person? If it's not my math teacher, then why, despite the fact that I applied deodorant seven times this morning, are my pits drenched with sweat?

"My vision is one in which all people from every walk of life can believe once again in the dream of America. In the promise that America holds for each citizen."

I force myself to turn my head and look at the person who I think is Mr. Applebaum. *It is him! What if . . . ?* I dig my fingernails into my palms and shiver. *What if Mr. Applebaum was the person who wrote those threatening notes? What if . . . ?* There are two policemen and someone from the Secret Service within feet of me. All I have to do is . . . But Mom was adamant that I wasn't to do *anything* to disrupt the convention. I was to sit in my seat beside Grandma until it was time to come onstage.

But if Mr. Applebaum wrote those notes . . . ? It makes sense. He had access to my backpack and could have easily slipped something into my locker. He knew how I did in the regional spelling bee. And he might have found out if I told Mr. Martinez about the threatening notes. Now that I think of it, Mr. Applebaum had been acting strangely for several months—always hunched over his desk, scribbling . . . *NOTES!* And once, after Mom won a primary, he squeezed my shoulder really hard. I didn't think anything of it at the time, but . . .

Mom would want me to tell somebody if she's in danger.

My stomach coils into a knot. I look at Grandma, hoping she'll see me, see the panic in my eyes. But her eyes are riveted on Mom at the podium.

Calm down, Vanessa. You're probably making something out of nothing. Mr. Applebaum is a nice guy. He's just a little strange because he's a . . . math teacher. Besides, he's surely here because he's a big fan of Mom's or a Florida delegate. There can't be any other reason. That would be crazy. All those times he was hunched over his desk, scribbling, he was probably just grading homework or quizzes.

I need to focus on Mom, but can't. I have a really bad feeling in my stomach. Maybe if I whisper to Grandma that my math teacher is in the audience, she'll . . . she'll . . . she'll say "So what?" and tell me to be quiet while Mom's giving her speech. What else would she say?

I tug on Grandma's hand. She looks down at me. I tilt my head toward where Mr. Applebaum is sitting and very quietly say, "That's my math teacher over there."

She looks in his direction.

Mr. Applebaum smiles and waves at Grandma.

She nods and turns back to Mom. "That's nice, dear, but pay attention to your mother. You'll have to go onstage soon."

My stomach feels like I just crested the top hill of a roller coaster and started the plunge downward. *I can't get up on that stage. The entire nation will see the enormous zit on the side of my nose. And besides, what if I trip?*

I decide to look at Mr. Applebaum one last time, to give

him a quick smile to show him that I'm glad he's here to support Mom. Then I'll focus on what I should be focusing on—Mom's speech.

But when I glance over at Mr. Applebaum, he's not watching Mom give her speech. He's glaring at me, a twisted half-grin on his lips. Then he pats his right hip. *What's THAT supposed to mean?* And winks!

I look straight ahead at Mom, and the creepiest feeling rushes along my spine. *What if Mr. Applebaum is the guy who wrote those notes after all? What if he really is planning to do something horrible?* I try to convince myself I have an overactive imagination. I tell myself that Mom will be done soon, I'll get on the stage for a few smiles and waves, and it will all be over. *It will all be over!* Sweat trickles from my armpits.

I glance over again. Mr. Applebaum raises his eyebrows and pats his right hip again. Is that a bulge I see at his waistband?

OHMYGOD! Somebody? I tug on my ear like crazy, as though Michael could send help all the way from North Carolina. I'm about to stand and point out Mr. Applebaum to the policewoman closest to me.

Then I hear Mom's preconvention instructions in my head: *Vanessa, don't do anything to embarrass me. This is too important. Just stay in your seat and—*

But Mom would want me to tell someone if her life is in danger.

My whole body is shaking. *If I'm wrong about Mr. Applebaum and I make a commotion, Mom will never forgive me. But if I'm right, I will never forgive myself.* I want to run onstage and wrap my arms around Mom and tell her my teacher is in the front row and is patting a bulge at his waistband. I want to be back in our house before any of this started. Before Daddy—

"Let's all work together to make America great once again."

OHMYGOD! Mom's almost done. It's nearly time for me to go onstage. I can't stand up there in front of Mr. Applebaum. I can't—

I force myself to look at him one more time. He's staring intensely at Mom. Too intensely. Then, like he knows I'm looking at him, he glances over at me and puts his finger to his lips, like he's signaling me to be quiet.

I want to tell Grandma what Mr. Applebaum just did, but I'm so scared I can't move. *He's not signaling me to be quiet—he's signaling me not to tell on him!* Mom said that anytime someone says I shouldn't tell on him, that's exactly when I should.

"Let's work together to make America a land of golden opportunity for everyone, not just the privileged. Let's . . ."

Oh, no! She's almost up to the part where I have to go onstage. After she says "God bless the United States of America," I'm supposed to count to fifty and then go up there and smile and wave like it's the greatest day of my life. *I can't smile and wave now!*

I turn to Mr. Applebaum. He grins at me; then his hand moves toward his waistband. *He's probably just reaching for his pocket to get a tissue, Vanessa. Don't jump to any crazy conclusions. This man is, um, was your math teacher, for goodness' sake. His nose must be running or he's sweating or—*

Mr. Applebaum reaches inside his waistband and pulls something out. My heart hammers so hard I can hear it pounding in my ears. I squint to see what Mr. Applebaum is holding. It's something silver and shiny.

"God bless the United States of America."

And he's pointing it at Mom!

I leap from my chair, barely feeling Grandma clutch the back of my skirt. I charge up the steps to the stage and pull free when someone grabs my ankle. "Mom!" The podium seems so far away.

When Mom looks at me, her face contorts. "Vanessa?"

I hear footsteps behind me. I wish the staff hadn't made me wear heels today.

When I almost reach Mom, the two things I feared most in the world happen at exactly the same time.

34

Mom stares at me, openmouthed, as my size gigantic shoe catches on a cord. I pitch forward at the same moment I hear an explosion. It feels like someone punches me in the derriere, and I'm thrown facedown onto the stage.

I feel someone throw himself on top of my back. *Mr. Applebaum?* I struggle, but can't move under the weight. The man's aftershave smells like Daddy's. "Giraffe is secure," the man whispers. "Giraffe is secure." *Giraffe? That's the Secret Service's nickname for me.*

A woman shrieks, and I strain to turn my head toward the crowd, but can't. *OHMYGOD! Where's Applebaum?* I'm able to turn my head toward the giant screen. On the screen, I see the podium and me lying in front of it with a Secret Service agent lying on top of me. *Very attractive!* There's one thing I don't see.

"Mom!" I scream, but only a croak comes out.

"Mommy!" I'm bawling now, unable to catch my breath with the agent's weight pressed on me. *Get off!* "Mommy! Where are you?"

As I'm being lifted from the stage, I barely hear the words "I'm here, baby."

35

The sickly sweet smell of flowers fills my room. But it's better than the way hospital rooms usually smell—like overcooked spinach and old pee. Flower arrangements sit on every surface: one on the rolling table by my bed, three on the windowsill, dozens on the floor. There are teddy bears lined up, too. And balloons and giant baskets of fruit.

"Who are they from?" I ask Mom. I'm still groggy from the pain medication they've been giving me.

She leans over and kisses my forehead. I notice that the rims under her eyes are red. "Well, Nessa"—it sounds so good to hear Mom say my name—"they're from people who care about you." Mom squeezes my head to her chest and sniffs. "Baby, you have no idea how grateful I am that bullet only grazed your . . . your . . ."

"Butt, Mom. The bullet grazed my butt. B-u-t-t. Butt." *Even though I made Mom explain what happened to me a dozen times, I still can't believe I was actually shot. Well, grazed by Mr. Applebaum's bullet before Secret Service and police tackled him.*

"I was going to say 'derriere,' Nessa. I know it only grazed your derriere, but it could have—" Mom's shoulders bob up and down. "Oh, Nessa, I'm so sorry. It's my fault. I—" She chokes on her words.

I've seen Mom cry only once before. And that was the night of Dad's funeral. At home. When she thought she was alone in her bedroom. I'm glad the Secret Service agent in the room with us now has the courtesy to turn his back.

Mom gently touches my hand. It reminds me of Michael's butterfly touch when I broke my wrist. "Vanessa," Mom says, "I promise I won't let anything like that happen to you again."

"Happen to *me?* Mom!" I sit forward, but the pressure on my injury hurts, so I lean back against the pillow. "Mr. Applebaum was pointing that gun at YOU! He was trying to hurt you. I just happened to get in the way when I tripped." *Thank God I'm clumsy.*

Mom bites her lower lip. "Nessa, it's my job to keep you safe. I failed. It's that simple. And I will *not* let it happen again."

I tilt my head. "What do you mean?"

My cell phone rings. It's on the table beside my bed. Mom answers it. "She's right here, Emma."

Emma's voice sounds so good, even though it's filled with panic. "Vanessa, when my mom told me . . . I couldn't believe . . . Are you okay?"

"Other than a really sore"—I glance at Mom—"derriere, I'm feeling pretty good."

"I can't believe it, Vanessa. I can't—"

"Honey." Mom taps her watch.

I scooch down in my bed and whisper. "Listen, Em, I've got to go, but I'll call as soon as I get home. Okay?"

"Sure. And when I get back from camp, we'll get together for a sleepover."

"Sounds great. I can show you my butt."

We both giggle.

"Vanessa?"

"Yeah, Em?"

"I'm really glad you're okay."

I let out a big breath. "Me too."

As soon as I hang up and start to talk to Mom, my cell rings again. Mom raises her eyebrow.

I mouth the word "sorry" and answer the phone.

"Hi, Michael."

"Oh, Vanessa."

"I'm okay, Michael. The bullet barely grazed my . . . my . . . derriere."

"You're sure you're okay?" Michael doesn't give me time to answer. "I watched you fall, Vanessa. I saw it on TV. . . . I mean, before they switched to a commercial. I was so scared. I thought . . ." Michael sniffs. "Did you get the flowers and teddy bear I sent? Well, that my mom sent?"

I glance at the rows of flowers and teddy bears. "I did get

them, Michael. Thank you so much." I catch Mom peeking at her watch. "Look Michael, I'm getting out later today. The doctor said I'm doing great and can leave. Can I call you when I get home?"

"Absolutely. Vanessa?"

"Yes?"

"Please take care of yourself."

My whole body tingles. "I will, Michael. Bye."

"A friend from Lawndale?" Mom asks.

I nod, and for some reason think of Reginald. "It was Michael Dumas. Probably the nicest boy at Lawndale Academy."

"That was sweet of him to call." Mom puts her warm hand on mine. "Speaking of Lawndale"—she pulls a giant card from behind my bed—"this is from Mrs. Foster and the staff. It arrived by special delivery. How she got them to sign this during the summer, I have no idea." Mom opens the card, and I see lots of signatures. The biggest one is from Coach Conner. He wrote: "You're one tough girl, Vanessa. Hang in there and get well soon. Looking forward to seeing you at school next year."

As if! I'm not looking forward to seeing you! "Mom, what school will I go to when you become president?"

Mom's eyes widen. "Honey—"

"Isn't Sidwell Friends the one Chelsea Clinton went to? Can we tour that school soon?"

"Nessa—"

"I know. I know. You haven't been elected yet. But, Mom, I've got a good feeling about this. I really think you will be. And we ought to start making plans. Right?"

"Vanessa."

"I mean, I'll need to find out if I can compete in the spelling bee when—"

"Vanessa!"

The agent in the room turns his back again.

Mom takes my hand. "Vanessa, Mr. Applebaum shot you!" She looks at me like she's expecting something.

"I know, Mom, but he's gone now. They caught him and he's in custody." *The thing I was most worried about happened and we survived!* "We don't have to be scared of him anymore."

Mom takes a deep breath. "Vanessa, there are a lot of Mr. Applebaums out there."

"There are?"

"I mean people like him. People who would hurt you or me."

"But, Mom—"

"And I simply can't take that chance."

"But, Mom . . ." *You said that even if we are afraid, we should do what's right anyway.* "I'm really not scared anymore."

"Well, I am." Mom leans close and whispers. "Vanessa, I gave this a lot of thought while you were in"—the word catches in her throat—"surgery." She lets go of my hand to wipe her eyes with a tissue. "Nessa, my number one job is to keep you safe. And I've let this campaign get in the way of that. I'm sorry." She bows her head, then looks at me again. Her nose is red. "I know . . . I'm sure . . . your dad would want . . ." Mom takes a deep, wobbly breath. "I've called a press conference for later today." Mom glances at the agent, then whispers in my ear: "I'm going to announce that I'm dropping out of the race."

36

"Mom!" I sit up, and wince from the pain in my derierre. "You . . . you . . . can't"—I whisper the next word—"quit! Have you mentioned this to anyone else?"

"No, I thought you deserved to hear it first."

"Thank God." I fall back on my pillow.

"Vanessa, I thought you'd be thrilled. Isn't this what you wanted?

"Mom." My voice is cracked and gravelly; my throat feels sore. I nod at the apple juice on the table beside my bed. Mom puts the straw to my lips and I drain the carton. "I did want that. I did. It's all I wanted before . . . I mean . . ."

Mom puts her palm on my forehead. "Shhh. It's okay, Nessa. You don't have to say anything."

I lean forward and take Mom's hand in my sweaty palms. "Yes, I do have to say something. Mom, I did want you to drop out. But now I don't."

"You mean—?"

I speak as softly as I can. "You can't quit! You have a really good shot, er, chance. If you're not elected president, who will clean mercury out of the water?"

"But I thought—"

"Mom." I grip her hand more tightly. "Who will work to keep guns out of the hands of people like Applebaum? Who will help that poor guy and his family from New Hampshire?"

"What guy?" Mom asks.

"Never mind." I flop back, exasperated. I can't believe I'm trying to convince Mom to stay in the race. It feels like it was only yesterday that I would have done anything to stop her. *Getting shot at certainly changes one's perspective.* "Look, Mom, you're so close now. You can't quit because—"

"Vanessa, I'm afraid for your life. And nothing is worth jeopardizing that." Mom clears her throat. "Not even the presidency."

"But you've wanted this since you were ten!" I run my tongue over my dry lips. "Mom, do you know what courage is?"

"Of course I do. Where is this going? I've got to get you checked out of here. And then there's the press conference where I have to announce—"

"Please, Mom."

Mom stops talking and looks at me. Really looks at me. Something she hasn't done in a long time. I swallow past my sore throat. "Mom, I realize you're afraid. I was afraid, too.

But I think this is one of those times when we need to have courage, when it's okay to be afraid, but we need to do what's right anyway."

Mom puts her hand over her mouth. "Oh, baby."

"Please promise me you won't drop out of the race at the press conference today. Please give it some time. At least think about it."

"Vanessa," Mom says, "I have thought about it."

I swallow hard. "Then be afraid, Mom." I swallow again; my throat is killing me. "But have the courage to do what's right anyway."

37

I squint in the bright sunlight. *I can't believe Mom gave in and allowed me to sit with her at the press conference. I can't believe I want to.* I sip from a bottle of cold water, grateful that someone left it on the table for me. Not only is my throat sore, but the air outside is hot, making me sweaty and thirsty. *Couldn't Mom have done this inside, where there is actual air conditioning? This humid weather is not at all conducive to a good hair situation.*

Mom points to one of the many reporters seated in front of us. "Yes, Bob?"

Bob stands. "This question is for Vanessa. How are you feeling?"

My stomach gurgles and I'm totally embarrassed. "I guess I'm a little hungry."

The crowd laughs.

"But I'm feeling great. My . . . it hardly hurts at all."

Mom smiles at me, then turns toward the reporters again. "Miriam."

"Thank you, Governor Rothrock."

I like the sound of that. But I'll like the sound of "President Rothrock" even more. Please don't tell them you're dropping out, Mom. Please.

"What happened to the shooter?" Miriam asks.

Mom nods to Mr. Adams, who is sitting on the other side of her.

"The shooter is in custody facing criminal charges," he says in a serious voice. "Franklin Applebaum became a math teacher at Lawndale Academy this past school year, we discovered, to get close to the governor's daughter and try to influence the governor's decision to run for president." *Franklin?* "He had no criminal record at the time he was hired. But in searching his home, agents discovered that Mr. Applebaum had a cache of guns hidden in a trunk in his attic, along with dozens of magazines about firearms. Mr. Applebaum did not use one of his own guns during the attempted assassination."

Assassination? Hearing the word sends a chill along my spine despite the heat. *I sat in that lunatic's classroom every day, worrying about whether or not I could draw a rhomboid!*

Mr. Adams is still talking, so I focus on what he's saying.

"They also found diary entries in Mr. Applebaum's home that prove he was vehemently opposed to the governor's views on gun control. Investigators uncovered dozens of threatening letters addressed to the governor's daughter near those diary entries."

I gasp. *He'd written way more letters than I actually received. It was a good idea to have a guard posted at my locker.*

"Unfortunately," Mr. Adams goes on, "we have discovered that someone from the local police department gave Mr. Applebaum the gun used in the assassination attempt. We are still trying to learn how he got the gun past security and into Mr. Applebaum's possession. That officer is currently in custody and facing criminal charges as well." Mr. Adams takes a swig of water, then puts his palms flat on the table as he says, "When Governor Rothrock is elected—"

Sweat is beading above Mom's upper lip. I will her to look at me. *Have the courage.*

"Governor Rothrock," a reporter shouts, interrupting Mr. Adams. "Since this terrible incident, have you considered dropping out of the race and staying home with your daughter?"

Mom presses her palms on the table and inhales.

Mr. Adams says, "Governor Rothrock has more resolve than—"

Mom holds up a hand, and Mr. Adams stops talking. "Thanks. I'll take this one."

She looks at me, and I smile at her. *Please don't quit, Mom.* I cross my fingers under the table. *Please!*

"What happened at the convention is very unfortunate. As a mother, I'm devastated." Mom touches my shoulder.

I realize my eyes are closed. I open them and see the crowd of reporters quiet, leaning forward. *Don't say it, Mom.*

"No one should see that happen to her little girl."

I'm okay, Mom. Applebaum is locked away.

"Someone like Franklin Applebaum should never have had access to a gun. But he did. To several of them, in fact. And that means one thing to me."

I'm crossing my toes, too, inside my shoes. *Do what's right, Mom!*

"It means that when I am president, I will work tirelessly to keep guns out of the hands of criminals. I will work tirelessly to protect not just my child, but all children." Mom smiles at me. "Of course I'm not going to drop out of this race. There's too much work to be done for our children's future."

I rocket out of my chair, knocking over my water bottle, and wrap my arms around Mom's neck.

"Nessa?"

I grab Mom's hand and thrust it into the air and smile like it's the best day of my life, just like I was supposed to do at the Democratic National Convention. I lean toward the microphone and say, "Rothrock and Miller. They're going to go all the way!"

OHMYGOD! Did I just say that?

Cameras whir and lights flash.

And I, Vanessa Rothrock, age thirteen and a quarter, let go of Mom's hand, pull out the sides of my purple skirt, and curtsy.

Curtsy. C-U-R-T-S-Y. Curtsy.

Mrs. Perez's DROP-DEAD Delicious Lemon Squares
(If Mrs. Perez isn't handy, get an adult to help
you with the oven work.)

1 3/4 cups plus 1/4 cup all-purpose flour
3/4 cup plus 1/4 cup confectioners' sugar
1 teaspoon grated lemon peel
1 cup margarine, melted
4 large eggs
1 cup granulated sugar
1 teaspoon baking powder
1/2 cup fresh-squeezed lemon juice

Directions

1. Preheat oven to 350 degrees F (175 degrees C). Grease a 9 × 13-inch pan.

2. In a medium bowl, stir together 1 3/4 cups of the flour, 3/4 cup of the confectioners' sugar, and the grated lemon peel. Blend in the melted margarine. Press the mixture into the bottom of the prepared pan and prick all over with fork.

3. Bake in the preheated oven for 18 minutes, or until golden.

4. In a large bowl, beat the eggs. In a separate bowl, combine the granulated sugar, the baking powder, and the remaining 1/4 cup of flour. Stir the sugar mixture into the

eggs. Finally, stir in the lemon juice. Pour this mixture over the baked crust and return the pan to the oven.

5. Bake for an additional 6 minutes, or until the filling is set. Allow to cool completely. Sprinkle the remaining ¼ cup of confectioners' sugar over the top. Cut into 20 squares.

6. Enjoy!

Dear Reader,

   According to the Constitution, only three things are required for a person to be eligible to become president of the United States:

   1. A person must be a native-born citizen of the United States.
   2. A person must be at least thirty-five years old.
   3. A person must have lived in the United States for at least fourteen years.

   That's it.

   To learn more about the Constitution, go to: www.archives.gov/national-archives-experience/charters/constitution.html.

   My mom ran in the primaries—those are elections held in each state to determine who gets to run for president during the November elections. When a person wins his or her party's nomination, a formal announcement will be made at that party's national convention. My mom won the right to run as the Democratic candidate in the national elections for president. A formal announcement of her candidacy was made at the Democratic National Convention before her big speech . . . and we all know what happened after that!

A fun place to learn about the government and the election process is: http://bensguide.gpo.gov/9-12/index.html.

For virtual tours, information about American history, and quizzes and games, try www.whitehousekids.gov.

You can also learn about Victoria Woodhull, the first woman who ran for president (fifty years before women were even allowed to vote), at this site: www.woodhull.org/victoria.php.

As you know, I'm a spelling bee aficionado. (aficionado—noun—fan; devotee; enthusiast.) Whether or not you compete in spelling bees, you can learn more about them by checking out: www.spellingbee.com.

I love playing Scrabble with my mom, even though she beats me every time.

But I'm getting better. In fact, I finally thought of a word that uses both the "j" and the "x": jinx—verb—to bring bad luck to. Too bad I didn't have an "n" or an "i" in my rack that night I was playing with Mom.

Did you know Scrabble was invented by a man named Alfred Mosher Butts? That's right: Butts. (Butts. B-u-t-t-s. Butts.) Mom probably wishes his last name were Derriere!

You can find out more about the history of Scrabble at: http://hasbro.com/scrabble/pl/page.history/dn/home.cfm.

For fun, try the Scrabble Dictionary or Word Builder at this site: http://hasbro.com/scrabble/home.cfm.

To learn about Scrabble clubs, tournaments, or the

Word of the Day, explore the National Scrabble Association at: www2.scrabble-assoc.com/.

One of my favorite books to help improve one's Scrabble playing is: *Everything Scrabble* by Joe Edley and John D. Williams, Jr.

That's it for now. Have fun! And wish my mom luck in the November elections!

Love,

Vanessa Rothrock

About the Author

Donna Gephart grew up in Philadelphia, Pennsylvania. (Go, Eagles!) When she was a kid, she loved riding her purple bike to the local library.

Today, she lives in South Florida with her husband, two sons, one cat, and a dog (who follows her everywhere). She still enjoys riding her bike and spends a lot of time at the local library.

Visit www.donnagephart.com to learn more.